THE BOOK OF
SECRETS

FORBIDDEN BOOKS, VOLUME II

DAVID MICHAEL SLATER

LIBRARY TALES PUBLISHING

PRINTED IN THE UNITED STATES OF AMERICA

Published by:
Library Tales Publishing
511 6th Avenue #56
New York, NY 10011
www.LibraryTalesPublishing.com

For general information on our other products and services, please contact our Customer Care Department at 1-800-754-5016. For technical support, please visit www.LibraryTalesPublishing.com

Library Tales Publishing also publishes its books in a variety of electronic formats. Every content that appears in print is available in electronic books.

ISBN-13: 978-0998333410
ISBN-10: 0998333417

For Heidi, always an open book.

"Meticulous, unmoving, secretive, he wove his lofty invisible labyrinth in time." ~ Jorge Luis Borges

CHAPTER ONE
Not a Bad Man

"Adem Tarik—Adem Tarik—I—I—"

"Here we go again," Dexter groaned, turning away from the early morning TV talk show he'd been half-watching. He shot an irritated look at his sleeping father.

"But it sounded like he was going to say something else that time," said Daphna. She hauled herself off the couch where she'd been slumped next to her twin brother and approached Milton's bedside. A glimmer of hope had surfaced in her speckled green eyes, but it faded when he failed to say anything further.

Daphna huffed and spun around.

"We need to do something, Dex," she said. "I think we should wake Dad and tell him everything we know."

Dexter's own speckled green eyes were skeptical. "But what if that makes him worse?"

"How could it?" Daphna said. "Besides, Latty will be here with his stuff from home soon. You've seen how paranoid she's getting again. Who knows when we'll get another chance?"

Dex closed his eyes. Up until a second ago, everything had been going fine. The trip from the hospital to the Multnomah Village Rest and Rehabilitation Home had gone off without a hitch and, more importantly, without a single mention of the name Adem Tarik.

Milton, worn out by the transfer, passed out the second he'd been settled into bed, so the twins had seized the opportunity to plop onto the room's guest couch and veg out in front of the TV. For nearly five minutes, they'd been able to relax. But now that exasperating name was on their father's lips again.

The surgeon who'd operated on Milton's broken hip said he'd been raving the name when the ambulance attendants wheeled him into the emergency room. He'd stopped when they'd administered the anesthetic before surgery, but then started again as soon as it wore off. Back in his hospital room, groggy on pain medication, Milton had kept it up, repeating the name over and over for almost two days.

"Adem—Tarik," Milton mumbled once again. Dex rolled his eyes, but Daphna put a finger to her lips. "I—I am—" their father continued, "I am not a bad man—I—Adem—"

"Hey!" Dex exclaimed. "That's what I told you he said in his sleep at home!"

Daphna thought a moment. "He's been blaming himself for being a bad father," she said, "for neglecting us all the time to scout books, like Latty told us. Or maybe he feels badly for not catching Mom before she fell in the caves."

"Or maybe there's something else going on," Dex protested. "We still have no idea why his mattress is stuffed with all that money. What if he did something illegal and feels bad about it?"

Daphna sighed. No matter how much they learned there was always something left to baffle them. But the suggestion that their father did something criminal was unacceptable. "If you think that, Dexter," she snapped, "then you should want to tell him what we know so we can get to the bottom of it!"

Dex rubbed his temples, which hurt. His whole face still hurt: black eye, split lip, and all. "Oh, all right," he said. "But he's probably going to have us committed."

Daphna shrugged, then turned back to her father, eager to ease his mind. She touched his shoulder with a gentle hand. "Dad?"

Milton stirred, opened his speckled brown eyes partway under their bristly gray brows, and murmured, "Um?"

"Dad, Dex and I want to talk to you. We want to tell you something."

"Hmrm," Milton murmured, drifting away already.

"We know the truth about Mom," Dex declared, now standing behind his sister.

At this, Milton seemed to rouse himself. His eyes weren't exactly lucid, but they were all the way open now. "What's that?" he asked.

Daphna felt sure they were doing the right thing. "Well—" she said, suddenly at a loss where to begin. "First we need to tell you about that book you were trying to get back from the ABC, the new shop in the Village that burned down. Where that beastly assistant knocked you—"

"Daphna," Milton said, "there are no new bookshops in Multnomah Village—or anywhere in Portland, for that matter." Then he fell straight back to sleep.

Daphna's face fell. He still didn't remember, and he wasn't pretending. A psychologist who'd come to talk with Milton in the hospital confirmed that. Her first theory was that he was suffering from an "adjustment disorder," which meant he was having trouble dealing with a recent traumatic event. Being thrown to the ground by a demented, red-eyed man-child certainly qualified, especially since he wound up with a broken hip and a concussion.

But when she learned that Milton had forgotten not only the incident, but also the events leading up to it, she said something more significant was involved. Given the endless repeating, it was more than likely something connected to this Adem Tarik.

Latty seemed to confirm this by sharing the history of the name. Dex and Daphna were there for the whole conversation.

"For many years," Latty told the psychologist, "the twins' mother, Shimona, had a rare book business in Israel. I was her manager and best friend." Latty stopped a moment, struggling to maintain her composure, but then went on.

"Just a few months after the kids were born," she said, "someone calling himself 'Adem Tarik' phoned me with a tip. He said some caves had been discovered in Eastern Turkey containing books far older than the oldest ever found before. He even gave directions. We didn't know what to make of it, of course, but we also didn't see the harm in investigating.

"Shimona, Milton, and I dropped the kids off with a friend and flew right there. We followed the instructions to a small opening in the side of some craggy hills not too far from a town called Malatya. We'd been inside for less than fifteen minutes when the caves started collapsing. There was an earthquake. Apparently, they're quite common in that area."

Latty acknowledged that going into those caves so unprepared, even going into that region of Turkey, was foolish and irresponsible, but she said bookscouts often did foolish and irresponsible things in pursuit of rare finds.

Of course, since becoming Milton's business manager and taking over as caretaker for the twins—and turning into the biggest worrywart of all time—Latty never did anything remotely like that again. She told the psychologist it was a miracle any of them survived.

"Milton escaped with a blow to the head," she said, "and

I collected more nasty bruises and cuts than I could count. But Shimona—she fell into a chasm."

Other than Adem Tarik's involvement, none of this was news to the twins. But there was more.

"We were all together," Latty continued, choking up, "the three of us, making our way along the edge of some sort of crevasse. Milton lit a torch, but he dropped it over the ledge when the earthquake hit."

"Go on," the psychologist gently urged.

"Milton got a hold of Shimona and me, but the cave floor was shifting," Latty said. "We all got thrown in different directions, and the next thing I knew, I was on the ground bleeding and couldn't get up. Some light was coming down from high above, and I could see Shimona. Her arms flailed as she teetered on the edge. It was so loud and chaotic and terrifying with rocks falling everywhere." Latty's voice went almost too low to hear.

"Milton desperately tried to keep Shimona from falling," she whispered. "He grabbed at her. It looked like he got a hold of her, but then a piece of debris hit him in the head. He was knocked out and—she fell."

Dexter and Daphna both stared at the shiny white hospital floor while they absorbed these alarming details, details kept from them all their lives.

Latty, struggling to hold back tears, managed to explain that when Milton came to, he didn't remember anything that had happened.

"Of course, he was told that Shimona was lost," she said, "but I didn't tell him how I'd seen him fail to save her. I never told anyone. It was so horrible. I dream about it all the time. Those flailing arms. It was like they were trying to fly."

Since Milton had hit his head on the sidewalk when he'd broken his hip the other day, the psychologist suggested that the blow might've triggered the return of all his dreadful memories, and that he was fighting to fend them off.

But when Daphna mentioned he'd been acting oddly even before he'd hit his head, she proposed that Milton's memories had begun returning on their own, something that eventually happened to a lot of people with traumatic events in their past. She thought maybe the new blow might actually be holding them back, so she asked Latty if there had been something very important to Milton around the time of the accident in the caves, something connected to the present.

Latty nodded. "Well," she sniffed, "in the caves, before the quake, we were talking about time, about how quickly it goes, and about how little time parents have before their children are grown. Milton felt quite strongly that children are really only children for thirteen years. He was telling us how he wasn't going to waste any of them and that he'd have a great celebration for the kids on their thirteenth birthday. And all this recent craziness did seem to have started when he came back just before they turned thirteen."

"That's very likely it, then," the psychologist decided. "The approach of the kids' birthday may well have punctured a hole in the dam blocking this memory. I'd say the second hit on the head is clogging that hole. Of course, I'm speaking metaphorically here. But if I'm right, it'll be a temporary obstruction. It's only a matter of time before the whole dam breaks."

That's when Latty's dam broke. She began sobbing outright. She said she'd do anything to save Milton from having to relive such horrors, but the psychologist said he had to if he was ever going to have a genuinely healthy mental life.

Latty was obviously not convinced, but she didn't press the issue. Instead, she walked unsteadily from the room with a wad of tissues pressed to her streaming green eyes. When she'd gone, the psychologist warned the twins not to pressure their father to see things clearly too soon.

All of this ran back through Daphna's mind as she looked at her sleeping father. She decided a little pressure was necessary right now. "Dad, think." She nudged him until an eye opened to her. "You brought a strange book back from Turkey. It was beaten up and full of all kinds of crazy nonsense words—"

"Daphna," Milton said, producing a patient but wavering smile, "I haven't gone to Turkey yet." His eyes, pools of foggy brown now, closed again.

"Dad," Dexter said, "Mom isn't who you thought she was."

Milton didn't reply to this, but he looked at his son.

"You're probably going to think we're a couple of lunatics," Dex added, "but she was old, really old—not like you, I mean." He hesitated, then took the plunge. "She was thousands of years old."

"Listen, Dad," Daphna put in, trying not to give her father a chance to tell them to stop being ridiculous, "I know this is all going to sound very weird. Just promise you won't say anything until we're totally done. Promise?"

"But it sounded like Dex said she was thous—"

"Promise, Dad!"

"Okay, okay, I promise."

"Good," Daphna sighed. "Right. Mom was part of a group, a Council, searching for a book," she said quickly, "a book that could someday show people a dangerous language called the First Tongue." Then she added, almost under her breath, "It's also called The Language of Power. It's sort of magic—or mystical, I guess."

Milton raised an eyebrow, but at least he was listening.

Daphna forged ahead. "See, there's this ancient myth that says God read from a book to create the world. No one knows if that's true," she hastened to add. "Anyway, it doesn't matter. The point is that people got hold of the book, early people. They used it to do good things for a while, but then mostly to wipe each other out. But the book kept getting lost, and eventually everyone forgot the language because it's really hard to learn and use."

"But somebody found the book again," said Dex. "And he tried to train a group of thirty-six child geniuses to use the language to bring peace to the world. Mom was one of them! He wanted to make Heaven on Earth. He taught the kids a Word to give themselves super-long lives so they could do it."

"But there was a war between the kids," Daphna said, "The War of Words, it was—"

Milton's eyes fluttered. They were losing him.

"Anyway," Daphna hurried, "the book wound up getting changed. The words, on the pages, they change. Mom did it to hide the language! She was one of those kids! So the Words of Power can still show up on the pages, but maybe not for a million years."

The eyes were nearly closed.

"But it got lost again!" Daphna shouted. "That's why Mom was searching for it! To destroy it once and for all!"

"But she finally gave up on the search to marry you!" Dex cried.

"But then she got that call that made you guys go to Turkey!"

"Dad! You found the book on your trip to Turkey this summer! That was it! That was the book everyone was searching for!"

"But you gave it to Asterius Rash at the ABC! He made

you! He was the kid who started the war!"

"But we got it back before the store burned down!"

"But Emmet, his assistant, got it from us in the park after all the Counselors were killed! They lived here! He's the one who knocked you—Wait!" Daphna cried, realizing she had some proof of all this. She fumbled her mother's letter out of her pocket.

"Dad!" she nearly screamed, "we found the letter Mom wrote before she went to the caves! Here, read it!"

But Milton didn't take the crumpled paper. He only looked at it trembling in Daphna's hand for a moment. Then he regarded his breathless children with a thoughtful expression.

The twins looked at their father with wide, anxious eyes, waiting.

Finally, their father spoke. "You kids," he chuckled.

Then he fell asleep.

Dex and Daphna tried to shake him awake again, but he was beyond reach. "Adem Tarik—" he muttered when they gave up and fell back onto the couch. "I am not a bad man—"

CHAPTER TWO
Food for Thought

The twins slouched back over to the couch, sank into it, and stared up dumbly at the TV. But no sooner had they settled in, when a voice called out urgently from the hall. "I'm coming! I'm coming!"

Latty.

She swept into the room, a frizzy-haired whirlwind of stress, hauling two suitcases, a grocery sack, and a shoulder bag with Milton's laptop. "Oh, thank goodness!" she said after casting a worried look over both the twins and their fitfully sleeping father. "It looks like you two have everything under control—not that I'm surprised, mind you." Without a moment's pause, she began unpacking and toting neat piles of clothes to the various dressers around the room.

"We're fine," Daphna said, trying not to sound as annoyed as she felt. "You said you weren't going to worry about us so much anymore."

"I know," Latty conceded. "But it's not easy."

"He started up again," Dexter said, dejectedly. "And now he keeps trying to say he isn't a 'bad man.'"

Latty looked horrified. "Listen, kids," she said, dropping some shirts into a drawer. "I don't care what that psychologist said. I don't think it would be good for your father to remember. I remember, and I've never put what happened behind me. It was too terrible. What I wouldn't give to forget what I saw! I don't think we should say anything, anything at all, about Adem Tarik, or the accident, or your mother. I'm so afraid of what it'll do to him if it all comes back. Listen, I want you both to promise me something."

"What?" both Dex and Daphna nervously asked.

"I can't be here twenty-four hours a day," Latty said. "When you kids are here, and he starts in on this...this nonsense, I want you to discourage it. Change the subject if he starts to realize what he's talking about. Okay?"

"Ah—" Daphna said.

"Um—" was the best Dex could do.

"Promise me."

"Okay," two sheepish voices agreed.

Latty tried to smile. "Everything will be okay," she said. "I'm sure Milton Adam Wax will be up and at 'em in no time at all." But this was hardly convincing from a world-champion fretter.

"What do you think Dad'll do?" Dexter asked, hoping both to change the subject and get some answers. "I mean, if he gives up scouting?"

"He's gonna need a job, right?" Daphna added.

Latty glanced at Milton, then turned to the twins. "I feel like it's been a million years since we've had a good talk," she whispered. "This feels good. I can see you two are worried about this, and that just proves you really aren't children anymore. I don't think we should have these secrets between us."

The twins snapped to attention. "Secrets?"

"Life can feel like a book full of secrets sometimes," Latty said, sounding rueful. "Best to be an *open* book."

"What secrets, Latty!" the twins hissed.

"Your father's a fine bookscout," Latty said quietly, "but he never made much money at it, not very often, anyway. It never really mattered, though. The truth is, he's rich."

"What?" both twins gasped.

"Shhh! Your mother left him a great deal more money than you ever knew."

"How much more?" Daphna demanded.

"Much more," Latty admitted. "If he didn't want to, your father wouldn't have to work for the rest of his life. And I'm taken care of too, kids, so don't worry about me, either."

In fact, the twins had never wondered how Latty was paid. They just knew she'd loved their mother like a sister and felt partly responsible for her death since she took that phone call and then got off so easy in the caves.

The Waxes lived in a fairly small house with nothing too fancy inside, though they had some expensive antiques. Multnomah Village was a nice neighborhood, but it was hardly the West Hills. There was rarely money for things like fashionable clothes or cell phones or summer camps—

"We're rich?" Daphna cried. She felt blindsided.

"Shhh!" Latty warned.

"You mean," Dex demanded, feeling blindsided, too, "that he's been ditching us all these years to search for books when he didn't even have to?"

"Please!" Latty begged. But she could see she had some serious explaining to do.

"Fine," she sighed. "Let's talk. But not here. We'll go to the cafeteria."

***

The trio sat down at the end of a long table. At the sight of all the food, the twins realized they were famished, but they were even hungrier for the truth.

"Okay," Latty said, sounding rather businesslike, "first, Daphna: Since you were a little girl, you've had an amazing will to succeed at everything you do. It's who you are. It's your very identity, and Milton never wanted to sabotage that. Wealth can change a person, honey. It's not uncommon at all."

For once Daphna was not the least bit pleased to be praised. This was completely unsatisfying.

Latty turned to Dexter despite the look on Daphna's face. "Dex," she said, "rest assured, your father never intended to neglect you. He was not wasting his time. The reason he spent the last thirteen years scouting has nothing to do with finding actual books."

"What do you mean?" Dex asked, trying to ignore the obvious implication that, unlike his stupendous sister, he had no will to succeed. Maybe he didn't, but that made it no less insulting.

"I mean," Latty said, "that what your father has been doing for thirteen years is searching for Adem Tarik."

"But—but, why?" Daphna asked.

"At first he was searching for information," Latty explained. "And I certainly couldn't blame him. In fact, I helped him. There were unanswered questions. No one ever took credit for discovering those caves, and no books were ever found, though I don't know how they could've been after the collapse. The name Adem Tarik was all we had to go on. Your father and I spent months looking for answers after moving here."

"How come you didn't look while you were still there?" Dex asked.

"That might have been easier," Latty acknowledged, "but I pushed for us all to move right away. Your father was in such a bad state. I wanted him to get started on a new life as quickly as he could, so I flew here to find a house a few days after the accident. Your mom had already sold her shop, so I never even went back to Israel from Turkey. You all came a few weeks later."

"If she sold her shop, why'd she go book hunting in the first place?" Daphna asked.

Latty shrugged. "I guess it wasn't completely out of her system. I wasn't surprised she wanted to go. Not at all."

"So, you never found out a single thing about Adem Tarik?" Dex asked, getting back to the point.

"Not one thing," Latty confirmed. "But believe me, we tried. Eventually, I let it go, but I couldn't get your father to do the same. I'm sorry now, but after a year or so, I encouraged him to consider scouting. It seemed like a good idea, even though it meant sometimes being away from you two. I thought the traveling lifestyle would be good for his health."

"His health? Was he sick?" Daphna asked.

"Your father was a picture of health before the accident," Latty said. "He'd never mention it, of course, but he was as strong as an ox. He could've run a marathon, even at his age. I'm not exaggerating."

"Dad?" the twins scoffed.

"Yes," Latty insisted, "but after the accident, he deteriorated. It was like his age caught up with him overnight. It wasn't anything medical, the doctors said. Grief can do that to you."

Latty paused to let a twitch pass over her cheek, and the twins could see plainly how fragile she was becoming. Her normally open, pink face was drawn and anxious. Her hair, usually kept in a neat bunch, was almost as out of whack as Dex's spiky mess.

"They say traveling is the best medicine for mourning," Latty continued. "To tell you the truth, I figured he'd settled into the job for its own sake years ago. He really did develop into a fairly decent scout. I wish I'd seen the signs better."

"What signs?" Daphna asked.

"Well, for example, after scouting for a few months, he set aside a large amount of money—scouts keep a cache just in case a deal comes along that won't wait for banks to open or checks to clear. The silly old-fashioned man stuffed his mattress with it." Latty smiled at the thought.

Dex and Daphna looked at each other, relieved.

"But he wasn't using it for that?" Dexter asked.

"I don't think so. I've always done the financial record-keeping, kids, so for that first period of time, I could see he was spending money on side-trips not related to the scouting itineraries I prepared. He was keeping up his search for Adem Tarik. I'm quite sure he really put the money aside so he could continue without having to endure my pestering him to get on with his life."

The twins sat absorbing all this, certain they'd turned no more than the first page of the book of secrets that was their life. But before either could think of what to ask next, Latty got up.

"Let's go check on your father," she said. "He's been alone for far too long."

CHAPTER THREE
Dirty Words

"It's that time again, everyone! Just say the word!"

"Wacky!" the audience shouted.

Dex and Daphna once again sat on the couch watching TV, or staring at it glumly, anyway. *The Anne & Anthony Show.*

"Righteo!" said Anthony. He was a man with a chiseled jaw and the fakest smile ever.

"Okay, we have a caller on the line," said Anne, the sculpted, bottle-blonde co-host. "Here's your Wacky Word—remember," she said, "if you define it correctly, you win! Anthony, why don't you do the honors?"

"Love to, Anne." Anthony flashed gleaming teeth at the camera and said, "Are you there, caller?"

"I'M PICKER!" the caller screamed, a man with the high, whining voice of a petulant child. Anne and Anthony, along with the entire audience, jerked back in their seats a bit.

"Whoa! Okay then, Picker!" Anne said. "We picked a doozy for you. Ready? It's—'Whackembackemphobia.'"

"Abracadabra! Make me famous!" Picker shouted.

Dex and Daphna looked at each other and smirked.

"Aww," Anthony said, "I'm afraid you only get one chance. 'Whackembackemphobia' is the fear of broken ribs. Children get it when Mom slams on the brakes and whacks them back with her arm to keep them in their seat."

The audience laughed. Lots of nodding heads, especially among the kids.

"Shazam!" the man cried. "I AM PICKER! MAKE ME FAMOUS!"

The twins snickered.

"Well, Picker," Anthony said, glancing offstage. "Best we can do is send you a couple of fine Anne and Anthony mini-statues. They're good luck! Hang on the line—"

"I always tell them," Picker said, whining now, "you gotta pick through a lot of garbage if you want to find a gem! That's why I work here! I do it on my breaks! Make me fam—!"

There was a click. Picker was disconnected.

Anne and Anthony looked at each other, momentarily stripped of their grins. Then they shrugged.

"And they say our show is trashy!" Anthony quipped, recovering his face.

"Well, like they also say," Anne added, "you can picker your friends, and you can picker your nose—but you can't picker your friend's nose!"

This joke was rewarded with gales of laughter from the audience.

Dex clicked the TV off. "What a freak," he said. "Shoulda tried 'Please.' That's the real magic word, right?"

Daphna, who'd been contemplating the stupidity of morning TV, was jolted by Dex's words. "Um, Latty?" she gulped, barely able to contain her excitement. "Where does the garbage from Multnomah Village go?"

Latty didn't look up from the drawer she was filling.

"Metro Central, I think," she said, "over in Northeast. Why do you ask?"

So Latty hadn't been listening. Daphna scanned the room, wracking her brains for an idea. "Dex and I are supposed to go see it. We're working together on a—summer project. We've been putting it off forever. It's due on the first day of school."

"But that's eight days away!" said Latty, alarmed. "That's not like you at all, Daphna. And right now is such a bad time to leave your father—wait a moment—did you say you were doing a project *together?*" Latty looked at Dexter, unable to hide her wonder at the very idea.

Dex hadn't the slightest idea what his sister was talking about.

"Yes," Daphna insisted, signaling to her brother with a significant look that this was important. "We're supposed to take a tour," she said, "and we're supposed to keep a journal of what we see. A *ledger,*" she added as forcefully as she could.

Dexter looked at the TV, then finally caught on.

"Yeah!" he cried. "It's my fault we haven't done it yet. Daphna's just being nice."

"Teal's in our group too," said Daphna. "Her mom's supposed to take us over there this morning."

"The girl that looks like you?"

Daphna nodded. *But prettier,* she couldn't help thinking.

The twins looked at Latty as she considered the matter,

worried she'd consider it all too unlikely a story. But despite how terribly anxious she seemed, after a moment, she smiled broadly and declared, "This is the best news I've heard in who knows how long!" But then a fearful look passed over her features again. "Oh, I guess I better not let my worries get in the way," she said. "Your father will be fine. But, please, kids, please—be careful."

"We will!" Dex and Daphna promised, already halfway through the door.

***

In short order, the twins were scurrying through Multnomah Village, dodging the multitude of ruts, crevices, and giant potholes in the mostly unpaved roads along the way. It seemed like all they did anymore was tear through these crazy streets. It would be much easier if there were decent sidewalks. Despite the constant threats to their ankles, they were home in less than five minutes, trying to catch their breath in the kitchen.

"'Abracadabra' and 'Shazam,'" Daphna panted. "They're probably real Words of Power if you say them right! Someone at the dump must've found Rash's Ledger!"

Dexter nodded, leaning on the table. "Thank God I threw it into a garbage truck!"

The moment Dex said this, Daphna realized why he'd thrown away Rash's collected Words of Power. He'd finally admitted to her that he couldn't read. So what good was the Ledger to him? She was sure he had the syndrome she'd heard about last year, a visual problem like dyslexia that made words appear all mixed up and moving on their pages. She'd been meaning to look it up, but she hadn't had the time with everything else going on.

"We've got to go out there," Dexter said.

"Let's take a taxi."

"Good idea. Do you have any money?"

The twins looked at each other.

Dex ran to his father's room while Daphna called a cab.

When it arrived fifteen minutes later, Dex held out a stack of bills to the driver and said, "How fast can this thing go?"

CHAPTER FOUR
Picker

For the following ten minutes, the twins—Dex white, Daphna green, both clutching door handles—watched Portland fly past their hurtling cab. The driver, whose license said his name was Herman Merk, seemed more than happy to endanger the lives of everyone in the vehicle. He went through five red lights, laughing at every squeal of tires and scrape of the undercarriage. But now he was finally slowing down.

It had been the most frightening ride of the twins' lives, but they'd asked for it. Slowly, their terror subsided, and they looked around at Industrial Northeast Portland.

Despite the fact it wasn't long past nine o'clock, large, lumbering trucks belching black fumes turned this way and that around them. On either side of the straight roads were large, dilapidated warehouses and dirty silos. A persistent hum seemed to vibrate in the air amid the sounds of engines and the scrapes and groans of massive bundles being raised or lowered on forklifts.

The cab bumped over railroad tracks. Then it crossed a bridge and approached a large fence with an open gate. As they passed through, the buzz behind them was drowned out by a tumultuous noise coming from somewhere on the grounds of the facility.

Daphna was just about to let Herman know he could stop when yet another noise reached them, the sound of panic. Seconds later, a mini-tide of terror-stricken workers, burly men in orange jumpsuits, flooded through the gate and rushed toward them.

Herman jammed on the brakes as the twins recoiled, but the men took no notice of the car. They fled around it as if running for their lives. Dex and Daphna turned to watch them bolting down the road. Just then, a bone-rattling collision rocked the cab, sending the twins crashing to the floor. When the car settled, Herman lunged through his door, bellowing. The twins, dazed but unharmed, followed suit.

An enormous piece of misshapen metal had been driven right through the hood. The engine was smoking.

Suddenly, something slammed and shattered on the gravel directly between the twins. It was, or had been, a stone birdbath. Dex and Daphna gawked at its carcass. Clearly, it would've killed one of them had it landed a foot away in either direction. Without a word, Herman turned and ran.

"What's going on?" Dex asked, unable to look away from the deadly shards scattered at his feet.

"Let's go see," Daphna replied, more prudently peering up into the sky. It was empty but for a large number of pigeons flying furiously away from the area.

Hesitantly, the twins walked in through the gate, past an empty booth and toward an immense warehouse. The riotous noise they'd heard at the gate was coming from within. Devastating crashes, the sounds of breaking glass and tearing metal, were shaking the walls of the building.

As they approached, something shot into view, a black streak, out of a broken window. Garbage bags. Dozens of oversized garbage bags streamed into the air and fell to the ground like fantastically swollen black raindrops.

Dex and Daphna watched the spectacle with nervous fascination as they moved slowly toward the entrance of the warehouse. Once it came into view, their attention turned toward the now nearly ear-splitting sounds coming from inside. It was dark and difficult to see, even with the jagged shafts of sunlight slicing in. What they could see, they could scarcely believe.

Objects of every conceivable shape and size thrashed around the unlit interior of the warehouse in the midst of a newspaper, cardboard, and plastic hurricane. Most of the inner walls had been felled in the tumult. It was as if a giant hand was shaking a snow globe filled with all the world's junk. Complete and total chaos reigned.

Entering would be suicidal.

A voice, barely audible through the din, cried out something incomprehensible.

"Someone's in there!" Daphna shouted.

"How could that be?" Dex yelled back.

The twins strained to listen, but just then, the pandemonium ceased. Everything fell to the ground as if someone had flipped a switch. Lighter objects, mostly sheets of plastic and newspaper, wafted around. It was the eeriest thing Dex and

Daphna had ever seen.

For just a second, everything was silent, but then the voice came again. "I AM PICKER!" it bellowed. "I will be famous!"

"It's *him!*" Daphna whispered. "He's got Rash's Ledger!"

"Famous!" the voice wailed. "Famous!"

Without consulting each other about the wisdom of the idea, Dex and Daphna stepped tentatively into the warehouse. The smell was repulsive, but they put it out of their minds and tried to head toward the voice. Between the paper and plastic fluttering all around, and all the other debris now strewn willy-nilly, it was nearly impossible to move anywhere with purpose, but they did the best they could, working toward the cry of, "Famous! Famous! Famous!"

The twins chose different paths, each wending their way over and around stacks of sheet metal, mounds of concrete and piles of paint cans, but neither seemed to get any closer to the source of the voice. Eventually, they ran into each other at the foot of a mountain of old tires. By then, both were covered in what looked like sheaths of laundry lint.

"This is impossible," Dex whispered. "I can hear him. He sounds close, but I can't tell—"

"I AM PICKER!" the voice roared. It was definitely coming from nearby. "I WILL BE FAME—What the—?" Picker's voice suddenly took on an entirely different tone, a terrified one. "Where did you come from?" he shrieked. "It ain't nowhere near Halloween you—Holy God! Is it yours? NO! I won't let you take—!"

There then came the sounds of a brief struggle, followed by an awful crack, after which Picker screamed, "AHHH!"

It sounded as if he took off running. He screamed as he went, though his high-pitched wail was interrupted every few seconds by the sounds of him crashing into or falling over something on the ground and then fumbling back to his feet. "AHHHHH!—ooomph! AHHHH!—ooomph. Oooooomph!" The wails grew louder as he got closer.

Finally, a reedy orange figure blundered around a blind corner and charged at the twins with his head down and one arm held awkwardly to his chest. He tripped and took a header right into them, and they all crashed back into the tires together.

Dex and Daphna clambered to their feet, unharmed, but Picker remained where he was, on his back, screaming bloody murder with his eyes closed. He clutched a twisted leg with his good arm.

"Are—are you okay?" Daphna asked, though she wasn't sure she could be heard over Picker's howling.

Picker opened his eyes. The sight of the twins seemed to stun him momentarily because he stopped wailing and blinked at them. Dex and Daphna blinked back. He was smaller than they were, and they were average-sized for thirteen year-olds.

"It's not right!" Picker whined. He tried to get up, but couldn't manage it. Instead he sank further into the tire mound and, red in the face, cried, "I found it fair and square! They can't mock me anymore. I am Picker!"

"Who can't mock you anymore?" Daphna asked, though she meant to ask if he was all right again.

"My *colleagues*," he answered, bitterly. "Always giving me the heaviest loads just to laugh at me 'cause I'm weak, always teasing me for picking through stuff to salvage for my collections. They've been calling me Picker for years. Well, I showed 'em how I pick 'em today, I did! You should've seen their ugly mugs! Scared to death, down to the very last one!" Picker grinned and tried to sit up again, but grimaced and had to lay back down. "It's not fair," he bawled. "That—that—huge *thing* took it!" Then, almost as an afterthought, he added, "It had no skin, and it stank a million times worse than anything around here."

Dex and Daphna looked at each other, alarmed. They were thrilled to have guessed right about the Ledger, but they knew this *thing*. It was Emmet, burned beyond recognition when he dragged his master, Asterius Rash, back into the inferno that had been the ABC bookstore.

And yet still alive.

"Who are you, anyway?" Picker asked.

The twins didn't get a chance to answer because they heard labored breathing nearby.

"Give me back my book!" Picker screamed toward it. "Give me back my book, you lump of foul deformity! Give me back my book!"

Dex squatted down and put his hand over Picker's mouth, stifling his cries. Crashes now came from the other side of the tires. Emmet was tossing junk out of his way as he came toward them saying something they couldn't hear clearly. Picker tried to bite Dex's hand, causing him to yank it away.

Picker opened his mouth to scream again, but Dex managed to whisper desperately, "He's coming to finish killing you!"

This had the intended effect, though the truth was that it would be Dexter and Daphna Emmet finished killing if he found them. Picker paled and remained quiet, but Emmet was starting to climb up the back of the pile anyway, repeating whatever it was he was saying as he went.

Dex and Daphna rose, ready to run, but just then the sound of sirens, many sirens, made them freeze. When they turned their attention back to Emmet's voice, it was gone. Dex climbed tentatively up the pile and quickly returned.

"Disappeared, didn't he?" Picker finally moaned.

"But, how?" asked Daphna.

"He just popped out of nowhere," Picker said. "It must be his book."

The sirens were getting louder, which seemed to please Picker.

"The cops are coming!" he cheered. "That means news!" He screamed something that wasn't English, and the tires began to tremble.

Dex and Daphna immediately jumped off.

"Picker, don't—!" Daphna yelled, but the little man called out the Word again, and tires started sliding off the top of the pile.

The twins knew they didn't have much time, so they headed quickly into the jungle of junk. Most of the debris had settled, which made it possible for Daphna to retrace her steps. Dex followed on her heels, having learned long ago to trust his sister's sense of direction. But soon enough, objects began to hurtle past their heads and shoulders. Brother and sister dropped to all fours and crawled the last fifty yards to daylight.

Once outside, Dex and Daphna got up and sprinted for the gate, but halfway there, they stopped. A gigantic and ominous creaking had sounded behind them. Turning back, they saw the entire warehouse lift an inch or so off its foundation.

It was impossible, of course, but so was everything else happening to them. The building hovered precariously in the air for one long, tense moment, almost as if it were trying to find the energy to fly away. Instead, it dropped to the ground.

On impact, the entire structure buckled, then collapsed.

The thunderous sounds of snapping beams rent the air,

then the blare of sirens cut through again. Three police cars and two news vehicles raced through the gate past the twins, so the pair tore their eyes away from the calamity and hurried forward into the nearby streets. They walked swiftly without talking for ten minutes, until they felt sure they were safe.

Daphna spoke first. "Do you think—?" she asked. "Picker—?"

"No chance he got out of there alive," Dex said. "But he's probably going to get his wish."

"What do you mean?"

"He's going to be famous. At least for a little while."

Daphna didn't reply to this. The twins walked for a while in silence again. All they could do was, literally, take this new death in stride.

Finally, Dex said, "Where are we, anyway?" He stopped to scrape off plastic and newspapers and the filmy lint still clinging all over him. They stood in front of a long fence topped with coiled barbed wire.

"Dex, Emmet is alive," was Daphna's response. "And now he has the Book of Nonsense *and* Rash's Ledger. And he can use some Words! That must be how he survived the fire! What should we do?"

"It's obvious," Dex said.

"What's obvious?"

"We have to get the Book of Nonsense back and destroy it. The Ledger too. There's no one left to do it but us."

Daphna didn't respond, but she didn't have to. Dexter was right.

The pair fell silent again.

"By the way," Daphna finally said, "I don't have the slightest idea where we are. Let's just walk until we see a cab."

The twins walked on, passing warehouses until they emerged from the industrial section. A taxi sat at a red light.

"Wait!" Dex yelled running to the car. The driver looked at him skeptically through her open window, so Dex pulled a handful of bills out of his pocket. She seemed mollified, if not exactly pleased. The twins jumped in.

"Address?" the cabby asked, still looking unsure about taking them anywhere. The license said her name was Sharon Ferry. Daphna gave it to her, looking nervously at Dex. Fortunately, Sharon turned the car in the direction of the highway.

Relieved, the twins pressed back into the vinyl seats and tried to settle their rattled nerves. It was almost a gift that increasingly incredible things kept happening because each new event prevented them from dwelling on the last.

Sharon turned on the radio. Classical music was playing, and Daphna found it soothing. "Lyre," she couldn't help saying. Dex rolled his eyes, but it was comforting for him, too. The twins sat and just listened for a few minutes, until Daphna's thoughts went racing again. "Dex," she said, "if that letter from Mom was important enough for Dad to keep in his mattress with all that money—I mean, he's been saving it for thirteen years—why wouldn't he read it? He looked at it like it was a prop we made for our crazy story."

"I don't know," Dex replied without much interest. "He doesn't even know what day it is. He probably just forgot—"

"Quiet," Sharon ordered. "If you kids are running away, or robbing people, I don't want to hear about it. Next thing you know, I'll be on a witness stand."

Dex and Daphna didn't bother to reassure her. They turned back to their own thoughts, which were the same: *How do you track down a giant, half-incinerated lunatic who wants to kill you? And more importantly, what do you do if you find him? Also, Are we really rich?*

A weather report came on as they drove over the river. The forecast was good, finally: sunshine. After that a newscaster said, "When we return, a review of breaking stories, including a disturbance at a rest and rehab home in Multnomah Village."

Blood drained from the twins' faces.

Sheer dread restrained the unthinkable from forming fully in their minds, but it was there anyway. Brother and sister couldn't even manage to exchange one of their by now routine looks of alarm. Instead, they clutched each other through an endless serious of inane commercials.

Finally, the news returned.

"In Southwest, at the Multnomah Village Rest and Rehabilitation Home, a large man clad in black and wearing a mask and gloves refused to leave when asked to state his business. He fled only when the director called the police, who are now investigating to determine whether this incident is connected in any way to the recent murders of several residents of the home."

Daphna let go of Dex's arm, leaving two sets of deep fingernail marks. She was indescribably relieved, so much so that she didn't bother wondering if there was still reason for concern. Dex was relieved too, but he looked worried.

"What is it?" Daphna asked.

"It was Emmet," Dex whispered. "He was wearing a mask—that's why Picker said something about Halloween. He must have taken it off to scare him."

Daphna, fearful again, sat back up. "What was he doing at the R & R?"

"Looking for one of us," Dex said, trying to keep his voice down. "He probably tried our house first, then went there."

"Those are the only places he knows I go," Daphna said, slightly relieved. "Does he know anywhere you—?"

Daphna stopped short because she and Dex knew exactly where they needed to go.

At the same moment, they asked the same question of their driver. "Can you take us to Gabriel Park?"

"If I don't hear another word," Sharon said.

And she didn't.

CHAPTER FIVE
Monsters

Dexter and Daphna stood at the head of the path lead-ing into Gabriel Park, wondering what exactly they thought they were doing. The last time they were here, the twins were fairly certain they were being led to their deaths. In that case, they'd had no choice, of course. Rash's old partner-in-crime, Ruby Scharlach, had a gun and the Book of Nonsense, and they had no idea Daphna's reading group was actually the seven remaining Councilors.

It was a miracle they came out of there alive, even with the Councilors giving up their lives to protect them. And now it seemed they were voluntarily going to risk their lives here again. They were going to walk right up to the thing that killed Ruby and took the book.

"He's been hiding in the woods—in my Clearing," Dex de-clared, trying not to focus on his fears.

"But how does he know about it?" Daphna asked. "How'd he find us there with the Dwarves—I mean, the Councilors. I shouldn't call them that anymore."

A vague memory came to Dex. "He—decked me, over there by that tree," Dex explained, "and when he left, I went to the Clearing to sleep. It's where I go when I skip school. I thought I heard noises in the woods when I was lying there all day, but I was too messed up to check. It had to have been him. He must've seen me go in."

A wave of hot shame swept over Dexter as he heard him-self describe his run-in with Emmet. He hadn't been decked, of course. Emmet had yanked him off his feet by the neck and nearly strangled him. He'd wet his pants—and it seemed like half the neighborhood had witnessed it. Dex had blocked out the whole incident as best he could, but he knew it was a doomed effort, even with all the insanity going on. And the humiliation wasn't even the worst part.

No, Dex had been forced to face a harsh reality that day: He'd never be the type of boy who did what he wanted—

he'd always be the type who did what he could. And learning that Daphna had wet herself when Emmet tried to murder her didn't help in the least. It made him feel even worse.

"What are we going to do?" Dex asked, forcing this all away. "Waltz in there and ask him nicely if we can have the Book and the Ledger? And by the way, please don't kill us?"

Daphna thought about this. Then she said, "Dex, I think I should go in there alone."

"What? Are you crazy?"

"I'm not crazy," Daphna replied. "It's just that—no offense, Dex—but I think I have a better chance by myself."

"But Daphna," Dex protested, "you lied to him, remember? To get him away from the store so I could take the Ledger. You flirted with him."

"Yeah, but I'm the one who made him remember he'd been happy in an orphanage before Rash took him and turned him into a killer. I saw the way he looked into my eyes, Dex, when he stopped choking me. I think I can reach him again. "Besides," Daphna added, "if Latty heard about what happened at the Dump, she'll be freaking out. She might even call Teal's mom. You should run back to the R & R and tell her we're okay."

Dex thought this was a terrible idea, even though Latty probably would be freaking out. Dex could hardly believe he was considering letting Daphna face that maniac alone. This was exactly what galled him. It wasn't that he was scared of getting hurt. Since the incident in the park, he'd taken Emmet's best shots, but he still felt ineffectual. He still felt that his own life was not his to control. He couldn't even make his own sister give an inch.

"Look, Dex," Daphna said, sensing some of what her brother was thinking, "I'm not going in there to fight him. Obviously, if I thought that was going to happen, I'd want you to go. I'm going in there so there won't be a fight. If Emmet looks even the slightest bit violent, I'll run for it. I'm not stupid, Dex. Let's make a deal. If I'm not at the R & R in an hour, you can call the cops."

Dex struggled with the semi-reasonableness of the plan. It was clearly their best option, but agreeing to it was still going to make him feel like a wimp.

"Dex," Daphna prodded, "we're wasting time."

"Fine," Dex finally agreed. "Half an hour."

"Deal." Half an hour was exactly what Daphna was bargaining for.

Dex regarded Daphna severely. He wanted to say something angry, but he couldn't find the words. Instead, he took off.

Daphna watched her brother until he was out of sight. After a deep breath, she straightened out her T-shirt, tucked some flyaway strands of hair back into her bob, then strode into the park with as much confidence as she could muster.

Despite the near state of shock she'd been in the last time she walked down this path, Daphna remembered just where Dex had led the group off of it. Chaotic thoughts swirled in her head as she entered the woods again. She hadn't found time to think any more about how she'd gotten Emmet away from the ABC that day. There'd been no time to lose, so she'd just charged up to him, hoping to come up with something—and the next thing she knew, she was flirting away like a Pop girl at school.

It wasn't something she'd planned. Daphna had no idea she was even capable of such a thing. She'd never been confident enough even to wonder. But now a cascade of tingles raced down her spine as she stepped lightly over clusters of branches and leaves. Everyone knew that girls who could order boys around earned the right to do the same to other girls.

But this thought nearly crushed Daphna. She'd always been one of those other girls! She'd been used! Wren and Teal, those twofaced Pop phonies. Those snobs. They'd lied about going away to camp for the summer so they wouldn't have to hang out with her. Those back-stabbing liars sat with her at lunch every few days and told her she was their friend.

Oh, she'd been a fool, a stupid, stupid fool. How gullible could she be not to have realized they buddied up to her only when they needed help with their homework? And what was her "help," anyway? Practically doing it for them. No, completely doing it for them. How could she have let that happen to her, especially when it was so obvious the way they manipulated everyone else!

The fury that had overwhelmed Daphna when she first realized she'd been blatantly used returned, though with far less self-pity. She hadn't had a second to think about how she'd fallen apart in her bedroom over all this, either. Daphna had no idea what she was going to say to those two when school started, but she was going to say something, that was for sure. An angry red haze clouded her vision, and she began knocking aside tree branches and kicking at rotten logs. Daphna completely forgot where she was going, but her feet found their way on their own.

By the time she reached the trees ringing the Clearing, Daphna was in a blind, stumbling rage. She barged right through a wall of overlapping limbs, stepped on something unnaturally soft, then tripped on something else that sent her pitching headlong to the ground. Daphna scrambled to her feet.

It was Emmet. Or something that used to be Emmet.

He'd been curled up on a blanket wearing a black sweatsuit. There were a pair of black gloves, a plain black ski mask, and a portable television lying nearby. Everything had tags still attached.

But now he was slowly getting to his feet. And now Daphna got a good look at what remained of his face. It was nothing but peeling crimson parchment. His hands and feet were gnarled, waxy, and wet, dripping with something that looked like puss.

Emmet looked at her tentatively, so Daphna tried not to look away, willing herself to focus on his eyes, his red, ruined eyes. They'd shaken her so much before, but now they were the least frightening thing about him.

"It's you," Emmet finally said, looking down at Daphna with what she could plainly see was simple shyness. No amount of damage to his face could conceal it. His voice sounded nervous, just the way it had when she'd lured him away from the store. "I was hoping to talk to you one more time, this time," he added.

"This time?" Daphna asked. Between Emmet's timid expression and his strange comment, she managed to forget her fear for the moment. "What do you mean, 'this time'?"

"This lifetime," Emmet replied. "Who knows if I'll even know you in the next."

"You sound like Rash," Daphna said. "I hardly understood anything he talked about."

"Rash only talked about one thing," said Emmet, "Time. The Infinite Quality of Time."

"The infinite quality of time?" Daphna repeated, dumbly. "I have no idea what that means."

"I can explain," Emmet offered. But before he began, he started shuffling around the perimeter of the clearing. Daphna used the opportunity to assess the situation. So far so good. She'd found Emmet, and he didn't seem to want to hurt her. Daphna scanned the area, searching for the Book of Nonsense or Rash's Ledger, but there was no sign of either.

Then it occurred to her that whatever Emmet was going to say might be worth considering. That is, if he had any idea what he was talking about, himself. It was hard to imagine a complicated phrase like, "The infinite quality of time," ever coming out of Emmet's mouth. But then, he probably heard something like it from Rash every day of his life.

"Time is forever," Emmet said, stopping his circuit directly opposite Daphna. "Think about that for a second." He paused and gazed up ruefully at the patches of blue sky visible through the branches over his head.

"There was no beginning to time," he continued, "and there won't be an end to it. And that means, even if it's ten trillion years from now, people will be born that look and talk and think exactly the way we have, which means they will be us. It has to happen, eventually. If time is endless, everything has to happen. Everything has to happen over and over and over again. We've had this conversation before, who knows how many times. I only wish it was my turn to kill Rash a long time ago, but I never thought of it. Maybe he could keep some thoughts out of my mind."

Daphna offered no reply to this, amazed now to see Emmet wasn't just parroting words he didn't comprehend. He'd obviously thought about what he was saying. When she'd led him around the other day, he'd just mumbled and stuttered like a moron, like the moron she'd assumed he was. Now she understood that he'd fumbled around her simply because he liked her and must've been nervous.

Daphna tried to refocus on what Emmet was getting at, but it was difficult with all these other thoughts crowding in. She was pretty sure she understood the gist of it, though. "Emmet, the world isn't infinite," she said, detecting a flaw in his thinking. "It was created at some point—one way or another—and it sure isn't going to be around forever. If we don't blow ourselves up, we're going to cut down all the trees until no one can breathe, or poison all the food and water supplies."

"Of course we will," Emmet agreed, surprising Daphna. "We'll do all those things." He began moving toward her, but stopped suddenly in the center of the clearing. Did she flinch, or look afraid—or disgusted? She couldn't afford to make him mad right now, not when she needed to get the books from him. Fortunately, Emmet didn't look upset, and he continued on with his lesson.

"Of course we will," he repeated. "I said *time* was infinite, not the world. The Earth will be destroyed, in every way you can imagine, but when enough time goes by, other Earths will form, just like the trillions that formed before this one. And when we—you and me and Asterius Rash—when we come around again, things will happen to us with ten billion tiny differences, or just one difference, or they'll happen exactly the same way. One time, Rash will adopt another child from the orphanage and brainwash him into feeling like an animal and force him to stare at books sixteen hours a day to find his stupid Words."

"But—"

"And another time, he'll adopt me again, and I won't practice every single Word of Power he makes me put in his Ledger—or I will, but I won't learn the one that makes you not feel pain, and so I'll die the same horrible death he did when the store burns up."

So that's how he survived. She tried to take in the rest of Emmet's lecture, but wasn't up to it. The nature of his words was confusing enough, but it was just too bizarre to be engaged in philosophical speculation here, in the middle of the woods in Gabriel Park, with a psychotic brute burned beyond recognition, one with a crush on her, no less.

And under the surface of this bewilderment her other worries simmered. There was her suddenly nonexistent social life, her ailing father and her insensitivity to her brother, not to mention the small matter of completing the Council's mission of finding and destroying the Book of Nonsense. Emmet was going on about infinite labyrinths of time, but Daphna didn't tune back in until his voice took on a much more subdued tone.

"One day," he was saying, his head bowed, his voice dropping low, "one day when we meet again, you won't have to pretend to like me." Emmet shuffled forward until he was standing directly in front of Daphna, who didn't draw away even the slightest bit. Emmet's voice sank to a whisper. "One day, when you ask me to walk with you," he said, twisting his singed fingers and trying to look Daphna in the eyes, "we might—maybe we might—hold hands."

The wistful look in Emmet's eyes—they weren't so ruined that Daphna couldn't see it— sapped her of every emotion but one. She felt horribly depressed. A sadness that seemed to have physical weight pushed down like the heel of a hand on her heart. She knew what she was going to do. She was going to play whatever feelings Emmet still had for her against him. What choice did she have? However smart he might actually be, he was dangerous—deadly. It didn't really matter that Rash made him that way, did it?

Resolved, Daphna smiled at Emmet. "One day you might meet me right here," she made herself say, giving her hair a flip like Wren always did, though she had no idea if bobbed hair could flip. "And you might give me the Book and the Ledger," she added, "as a sign of the friendship we're going to have next time." Daphna tried to enlarge her dappled eyes the way the woman on the TV talk show had when she looked at the camera.

Emmet returned a forlorn, exhausted smile, but didn't reply at first. As Daphna waited nervously for his response, it occurred to her that his gruesome appearance no longer bothered her, but before she had time to figure out what that meant, Emmet let out a bleat of surprise and then abruptly collapsed like a marionette whose strings had all been severed at once.

Daphna dropped to her knees beside him. "What is it, Emmet?" she pleaded.

"Crap," Emmet grunted, rolling carefully onto his back.

"What's wrong?" Daphna asked. "Are you okay?"

"Doesn't hurt, but I guess I'm all burnt up inside."

"Do you know any Words to help?"

"Maybe." Emmet screwed up his eyes, thinking. Then he started intoning a series of odd-sounding Words. They sounded similar to those Daphna heard Rash use under his breath at the ABC.

Suddenly, leaves swirled around them, lifting off the forest floor in a mini-twister. Then bark peeled off a stand of trees across the way. Behind her, Daphna could hear branches swaying as if in heavy wind, but she didn't turn around because Emmet rose unsteadily into the air, the same way the Metro Central's warehouse had. But then he quickly sank back to the ground. Terrified, Daphna just sat there next to him as the fluttering leaves settled on her head and shoulders like discarded scraps of paper.

"It's no use," Emmet sighed. "I'm too messed up. I think my brain's been cooked."

"Think! Emmet," Daphna urged, forcing herself to focus on her mission. "Do you know anything else?"

Emmet closed his eyes. His hairless brow furrowed with concentration. Finally, he muttered a Word that sounded like he was spitting out something distasteful. The moment he did, Daphna couldn't breathe. She clutched her throat, and when Emmet saw her, he repeated the Word and then fell silent. Daphna gasped as the air flowed into her again.

"I'm sorry," Emmet whispered. "It's no use—" He looked Daphna firmly in the eyes and said, "I was hoping this life was going to come around. I was sure you were going to make me good. That's why I was looking for you. Can you make me good?"

"I—I—it's okay, Emmet." Daphna's eyes welled up. It was impossible to know exactly what she was feeling. She took Emmet's hand. It felt a little bit like the cover of the Book of Nonsense.

"You don't have to pretend anymore," Emmet whispered. His voice was soft, almost gentle. "There's no possible way any of my future lives can be worse than this one."

"But I'm not pretending," Daphna pleaded. It came out as a whine. Tears swam before her eyes. She was lying to a dying boy. Or, if she wasn't lying, she wasn't telling the truth, either.

"I believe you," Emmet croaked, his voice cracking now, his eyes beginning to roll in their sockets. "You can have the books," he said. "I was going to give them to you when I was done with them, anyway. I only learned to use a few Words in Rash's Ledger, but you're smarter. It's the first Word that chokes people. The last one on the fourth page lets you go wherever you want just by thinking about it. I only got it to work a few times."

"That's what you did at the dump!"

Emmet nodded weakly and waved at something across the way.

"They're over there, under that split log," he said. "I don't think that other book will do anything for you, the one I got back from that old lady. It's all messed up and full of nonsense. I took it 'cause Rash was desperate for it. I thought it might have something in it I could use to change my skin back, but it's useless. That's why I went after the Ledger, except I couldn't find anything to help me in there either. I didn't have enough time." Emmet couldn't help but laugh at the irony.

"Thank you, Emmet," Daphna said, softly. "I need to ask you something else." There was no turning back. She was going to work her advantage as far as she could. "Do you know anything about someone called Adem Tarik?"

"Rash talked about him all the time," Emmet said.

"He *did*? What did he say? Emmet! What did he say?"

Emmet looked surprised by Daphna's ferocity, but he answered without questioning her. "Rash was obsessed with finding some kind of magic book that used to belong to Adem Tarik," he explained. "He'd freak out at least once a day and start screaming about how Adem Tarik was a fool for wanting to make Heaven on Earth. Sometimes he'd laugh, but mostly he'd just scream. I kept away from him when he did that. I guess he thought that book over there was it. I don't know."

Daphna's mind spun. This was critical information, but she couldn't think why just then. "Emmet!" she cried. "Emmet! Is there anything else?"

Emmet's eyes had closed again, clearly against his will. But because he wasn't actually suffering, it seemed as though he was just exhausted and unable to keep from falling asleep, like Milton. Daphna knew better though, and after several more urgent pleas, Emmet seemed to revive.

"Sorry," he managed. "Rash told me he stole the book, but he lost it somehow. When we came here, he told me the thirteen-year-old he was looking for had something to do with it. He told me if I found the kid, he'd let me kill someone. But now that I've killed two, I don't feel any better."

"Is that it?" Daphna asked, aware but unable to acknowledge the seething volcano of regret under the surface of Emmet's words. "Did he say anything else? Hold on, Emmet!" Daphna insisted. She knew most of this. She knew Rash had come for one of her mother's children to learn the Words of Power for him. She needed more.

"I'm okay," Emmet muttered weakly. His eyes opened to Daphna once again. They seemed to clear out completely, if only for a moment, and he said in a determined voice, "Next time. Next time I'll do better."

Then, without shudder or complaint, he let out a long, slow breath, closed his eyes, and went utterly still.

CHAPTER SIX
More Monsters

Carefully, Daphna set Emmet's hand down. She said his name, but he didn't reply. She touched his shoulder, but he didn't react. He looked peaceful now, and for that she was glad.

"I'm so sorry," Daphna sighed, and her eyes finally overflowed.

But she got up, angry at her tears. Why should using her new talent, a talent she'd never dared dream of having, make her feel so awful? *You did the right thing,* she told herself, wiping her face. *You had to get the books, and you got them the only way you could.*

Maybe she felt sick because it made her like Wren and Teal, but she'd done a good thing here, an important thing. It wasn't like she was getting some moon-eyed boy to carry her books. That had to make a difference, didn't it? She wasn't anything like those girls, no matter how much she looked like one of them.

Daphna hardly knew who she was anymore. She paced the perimeter of the clearing, trying to puzzle things out. The only thing she understood was that she didn't understand anything anymore.

But then she had it.

Emmet had already told her everything she needed to know.

"Well," Daphna said right out loud—she felt better even before the words passed her lips—"next time, I'll do better, too."

Suddenly, Daphna could focus on the matter at hand. She approached the log Emmet had gestured to and crouched down beside it. Despite its size, it rolled over easily, revealing a cavity below. They were right there, the mutilated Book of Nonsense and Rash's Ledger.

Thousands and thousands of years of searching, of fighting, of killing were over. Daphna, daunted by the epic story she'd joined, didn't reach for either book, but rather remained where she was, staring at them, lost in thought about time. Could time really be infinite? How could it not be?

She'd first learned about the concept of infinity in elementary school, when one character in a cartoon movie asked another to think of the biggest number he could and then told him to add one, and then add one again, and then add one again, on and on.

Well, Daphna thought, *if the world ever ended, there would still be a moment after that, and one after that, even if no one was there to experience it, right? And as for the first moment of the world—there still had to be a moment before that, and one before that, forever the other way.*

Daphna didn't know what any of it meant. She took a seat, shaking the entangling web of thoughts away. Finally, she reached out for the precious books. After lifting them out of the hole, she tenderly whisked the dirt off their covers and set them on her lap. She'd looked through the Book of Nonsense before, or tried to anyway, when she and her father were taking it to the ABC, thinking it was just a very strange book that might have some value despite its mangled condition. It had been interesting then, but now it inspired absolute awe. It was hardly a book of nonsense. This book contained the secrets of a supernatural power. *Could a book really belong to God?* Daphna didn't know the first thing about the subject, but anything seemed possible at this point.

Carefully, Daphna turned over the nearly shredded cover and looked at a random page. The words were a blur, even more so than they'd been when she'd opened the book with her father and figured she'd gotten carsick. The words were now in rapid flux, and they dizzied her.

She flipped forward, but all the pages looked that way, so she closed it and opened the Ledger instead. Inside its pages were neat lists of fairly legible words. They didn't have explanations, but Daphna didn't find that troubling. They were Words of Power—the closest thing to them, anyway—and they were right there, for her eyes only, thanks to Asterius Rash's centuries of dogged hunting and collecting.

Daphna tried the first Word, the one Emmet had accidentally choked her with, but nothing seemed to happen. She paged through, scanning the lists, trying various Words in a low voice. After a particularly strange one, the Ledger slid to the edge of her hand, paused, then fell to the ground. It didn't work when she tried again, so she closed the book.

Amazed, and not a little terrified, Daphna closed her eyes and sat motionless but for her trembling hands that cradled the books. Her reverie did not last long, though.

Voices.

People were in the woods nearby.

Daphna got to her feet, took one last guilty look at Emmet lying in the center of the clearing, then rushed back toward the park.

Just before emerging from the woods, Daphna veered behind an especially large cedar tree with the two books clutched awkwardly under an arm. A group of fifteen or so boisterous girls were playing Frisbee on the adjacent grassy field. She recognized most of them from school: Ava, Branwen, Jarita, Robin, Yara. They were Pops: the best dressed, the best talkers, the best looking.

Daphna had never claimed to be super close friends with any Pop, but it wasn't like she couldn't go up and talk to each and every one of them. Even if Wren and Teal were liars and users, the rest of them were nice to her, and she didn't do their work for them.

Still, Daphna didn't want to deal with any Pops just yet, so she moved stealthily back into the woods and walked along behind the border of trees. When she felt she was beyond the girls' field of play, Daphna reentered the park, but after no more than two steps, an errant Frisbee hit her smartly in the back of the knee. The books tumbled out of her hands onto the grass.

Daphna was bending down to gather them up when someone called, "Little help!" She cringed at the nasally voice. Wren. And Teal was surely half a step behind because the two were practically joined at the hip. Their possible presence was the real reason Daphna avoided walking through the game. She wasn't remotely ready for this confrontation. Having no choice, Daphna stood up and turned around when the girls reached her. They looked momentarily stunned in their matching sun visors.

"Daphna!" Wren cried, breaking into a gleaming, perfectly orthodontured grin. She sounded for all the world like she'd just run into her long-lost bestie.

"How was camp?" Daphna asked, coldly. She felt like she was a thousand years older than these twits now. How could she ever have admired them?

"Oh, it was awesome," Wren lied, her blue contact lenses shining with wonder at all the fake memories. "Really, you should come next year. It would be so cool to hang with you."

"I thought you weren't getting back until next week."

"Oh, yeah," Teal said. "Um, well—"

"There was a fire!" Wren lied. She barely even paused before coming up with it. "They had to send us home early. That was a bummer, but it was kind of cool in a way. We heard there was one around here too. We were all just talking about it. Did you see it?"

Daphna seethed thinking of the letters she wrote while waiting for them to send the camp's address. "I know you didn't go to camp," Daphna snarled, suddenly too furious to go on with the charade. "I know you've been using me."

Wren and Teal looked at each other.

"It's nothing personal," Teal said after a long, hideously awkward pause during which Daphna's heart pounded furiously in her chest. "We just—in the summers, we're really too busy—"

"To keep stringing me along," Daphna said. "Yes, I see. Lots of Frisbees to throw. Also to catch. And putting together the Frisbee outfits. I'm sure it's all quite overwhelming."

Wren smirked. She didn't look interested in offering any excuses. She looked amused, if slightly surprised. "We figured you were busy doing next year's homework, anyway," she said. "I'll drop mine off tomorrow."

"Let's go, Wren," Teal said.

Daphna's face felt like it was ready to catch fire. "I can't believe I ever wanted to be your friend," she fumed. "I can't believe I didn't see how pathetic you two really are."

"You calling us pathetic?" Wren laughed. "Now that's pathetic!"

"Come on," Teal urged, looking back at the others. "She's not worth it."

"You have no idea what I'm worth, you—you—twit!" Daphna raged.

Now Teal's eyes went narrow. "You might as well know," she said, her voice a bit shaky, "that every single person over there knows what a sucker you are. We all used to take turns saying something nice to you to make sure you'd keep the answers coming."

"Everyone is going to be so disappointed," Wren put in, pleased her partner was finally joining the fun. "But then again, there's never a shortage of wannabes. By the way, love the outfit you put together."

Daphna looked down and saw that she was covered in clots of that lint-like junk from the dump, and now leaves and twigs were in her hair from the clearing too. And despite the fact that her appearance demonstrated just how much distance there was between her concerns and those of these two shallow, spoiled little prima donnas, she was ashamed.

Ashamed of being ashamed, humiliated and incensed, Daphna simply wanted to scream. And she did scream, but what came out was some kind of incomprehensible word.

The moment it passed her lips, Wren and Teal doubled over, blue-faced and choking.

Daphna, shocked at first, stared down at them in confusion. When she finally grasped what was happening, she was too flustered to make it stop. Teal's eyes bulged incredibly from their sockets. Wren clutched her chest and tried to scream. They both fell to their knees and looked up at Daphna, terrified.

Daphna gaped down at the strangling girls, less flustered now than simply amazed. Thank goodness they were both thirteen and able to hear the First Tongue. They were literally groveling at her feet. In her wildest revenge fantasy—not that she'd had time to actually formulate one—she'd never have dared hope for such a thing. Wren fell on her face and clutched at Daphna's shoe.

Enough was enough, though. It took several tries, but Daphna managed to pronounce the Word again. Immediately, the girls rolled onto their sides, sucking in air. The moment they could, they got back to their feet and, massaging their throats, staggered away without their Frisbee.

Daphna watched the girls rejoin the other Pops before tucking the books back under her arm and heading off. Did any of that just happen? Shouldn't she be feeling a whole lot worse if it did?

Next time, Daphna told herself, *next time I'll handle things better.* But she had to say this repeatedly in her head as she walked. It was the only way to drown out the other little voice in there, the one telling her that if she lived forty billion lives, she'd never want to handle it any other way.

CHAPTER SEVEN
Mixed (Up) Messages

Second thoughts gnawed at Dexter as he sprinted away from the park. It was he, not his sister, who should've gone into the woods. Yes, Daphna had logic on her side, but he was a boy. She was a girl. But that was stupid, wasn't it? Dex didn't know. He did know he'd get nothing out of Emmet if he went in, except possibly two oversized hands around his throat that wouldn't let go until he was dead. He wasn't going to confuse his newfound ability to take a punch with committing—

The blaring of a furious horn made Dex suddenly stop. Only when the car passed did he realize he'd charged blindly across a street—and how close he'd come to being flattened. Dex leapt onto the opposite sidewalk and stood there hunched over with his hands on his knees, trying to steady his fraying nerves.

I should go back, Dex thought when he recovered, but then he looked up to find he was standing right outside the R & R. There was only one thing to do, it having actually been too late to change the plan for nearly ten minutes. He sped in through the Home's automatic doors, hurried across the lobby, and burst into his father's room.

"What's going on?" Latty yelped. She was sitting in a chair pulled up next to Milton's bed. He was propped up with his laptop on the food tray, looking surprisingly refreshed and alert.

At first, Dex thought Milton must've told Latty the story he and Daphna told him and she was furious they'd gone against her wishes. But his father didn't look concerned at all.

Then Dex realized how his entrance must have looked. He still had some of that fluffy junk from the dump stuck to his clothes, and he was sweating profusely. "Nothing's going on," he said, "just thought you might be wondering where we were." When Latty looked confused, he added, "There was an—accident at the dump, but we were nowhere near it. There was all this stuff there—couches with their insides all pulled out—we were messing with it."

"An accident?" Latty cried through the hand that shot to her mouth. Then, inexplicably, her face purpled and she began to cry.

Dex had no idea what to say. Latty was clearly going to pieces. He glanced at his father, who returned a knowing look. Dex had no idea what it meant. "Ah, hey, Dad," he offered. "How's it going?"

"Hi Dex," Milton said. He sounded quite cheerful, though his voice was hoarse.

Latty stood up. "If you're here to keep your father company," she sniffled, pulling herself back together, "I may just run home to get the house organized and start working on dinner. The kids will bring you something later tonight, Milton. That lunch they wheeled in here was criminal. Is Daphna home?"

"She's coming here in a bit."

"I hope she hurries," said Latty, voicing Dex's thoughts, precisely. "I feel much better when you two are here with your father, safe and sound." Then she added, with an only half-joking wink, "You two can protect him from that Evelyn woman."

Milton rolled his eyes good-naturedly.

After extracting a few tissues from her purse, Latty hurried out, though not before pausing to brush and straighten Dex's shirt. When she had him by the collar, she leaned over and whispered, "Don't forget what you promised." Then she straightened up and hurried out the door.

Dex looked at his father, unsure what to say next. "What's wrong with her?" he managed.

"Oh, you know Latona," Milton said with a tolerant shrug. "If you think she worries over you guys too much, you don't know the half of it. Trust me."

"But why does she have to worry so much? It doesn't seem healthy."

"You two are her life," Milton said, "and you're all she has of your mother. In fact, it was Latty who talked her into trying to have kids in the first place. Your mom thought she was too old. And of course Latona has no family of her own—"

Dex had never considered Latty's personal life. He'd assumed she had some kind of family, somewhere, though she clearly didn't ever see them now that he thought about it. Of course, neither he nor Daphna had extended family, either. Maybe Latty was trying to make up for all that. "What's she got against the lady who runs this place, anyway?" he asked.

Milton chuckled. "Just like they say," he said, "the more things change, the more they stay the same."

"What do you mean?"

"Oh, well, do you remember how I met Evelyn? I guess how we all met her, really. You and Daphna were with me, after all. We all sat together on the same flight from New York to Portland. We'd connected from Jerusalem, and she was moving from New York City.

"Anyway, I guess she took a liking to me, and to you two, as well. Latty could see this when we all walked off the plane together, or at least when she saw Evelyn give me her phone number. The truth was I found her a bit aggressive for my tastes. Anyway, Latty took an immediate dislike to her."

Dex struggled to keep a straight face. A woman hitting on his father? The very idea was laughable. The story was over, but he didn't know how to keep the conversation going. It seemed his father didn't either.

After an awkward silence, Milton said, "Oh! How could I have forgotten? Latty tells me you and your sister are collaborating on a project about city waste."

"Ahh—"

"It just so happens I know someone who used to have an interesting history of garbage if you're interested—my old friend and colleague Berny Quartich. The odder the topic, the more likely he is to have the perfect book about it! Since I woke up I've been feeling fantastic, other than the sore throat and strange dreams, anyway. So when Latty told me what you were up to, I e-mailed him. He already wrote back and said he still has it. Here, have a look."

Panic shot up in Dex like a geyser. He was nowhere near ready to tell his father about his reading problem. He wasn't so sure about this syndrome thing. Daphna probably didn't remember it right.

"Ah—sure," Dex stalled, "but you said you're having strange dreams?"

"Yes," said Milton. "One, actually."

"What is it?"

"I keep dreaming that I'm walking down a stone street in Malatya—"

"That town in Turkey you went to!"

"I've been there before," Milton said, "but not for some time. I'll be going this summer, actually, so I guess it's on my mind."

"Okay," said Dex, deflated to see there'd been no change in his father's memory. "So what happens?"

"Well, I do know the town, but not this street. It's not along the main area of commercial or industrial activity. It's lined with quiet little shops."

"Do you go in one?"

"Yes, a coffee house, the kind where they read your fortune in the grounds of your cup. Fikret Cihan's Coffee House. I just remembered that."

"Weird," Dex said. "You don't even drink coffee." He was beginning to suspect that this was a memory, not a dream. "Do you get your fortune read?"

"No," Milton said. "I ask the proprietor, Fikret Cihan, about an author I'm curious about. He tells me he hasn't heard of him, but then suddenly someone I hadn't seen in the back of the shop, an ancient looking old fellow sitting under a lamp copying text from a book, lets loose an awful, soul-piercing cry. He falls out of his seat with the book he was copying and literally begins crawling toward me with it. There is all kinds of confusion in Turkish, but eventually this Fikret brings me the old man's book and begs me to take it away that instant. It's in awful shape."

"Then what?"

"Well," Milton said, looking slightly taken aback by Dexter's enthusiasm, "I take it, give him my card, and walk back outside. And that's the end of the dream."

Dex, certain now that this was how his father found the Book of Nonsense, decided to take a risk. "This author, Dad, that you were asking about—"

"I don't think it's an important detail, Dexter. I can't actually remem—"

"Any chance it was Adem Tarik?"

Dex held his breath.

"That name," Milton said, knitting his brow, "it does sound familiar. Where did you hear it?"

"Um," Dex said, "you said it when you were sleeping."

"Perhaps that was it then. But enough of this nonsense," said Milton. "It's you I want to talk about. I'm ashamed to say there's so much about you I don't know. I really would like to help with your project. Shall we respond to this e-mail?"

"Actually, Dad," Dex said, "we've decided to change our topic."

"Oh, to what?"

"We're not sure," Dexter replied, but he'd seized on an idea. "Maybe you can help. We're supposed to interview someone in an unusual line of work, and I was thinking—"

"You—you don't mean you want to interview me, do you?" Milton asked, misunderstanding. His eyebrows had piled up, and his lips were parted in surprise. "Don't tell me after all this time, you've finally come around—"

"Bookscouting is pretty cool," Dex said, feeling a sharp stab about how pleased his father looked, about how easy it would've been to show just a little interest all these years. "We'd like to interview you," he lied, struggling to keep the conversation turning to his purpose, "but you gave me another idea. I'm thinking it can't get any more unusual than reading fortunes in a Turkish Coffee House. How 'bout we check to see if there really is a Fikret Cihan's Coffee House in Turkey?"

"Well," Milton said, "why not? Let's see what we can do." He clicked around on his computer and opened up a search engine. After a moment he said, "Well, I'll be. There is. In Malatya, Turkey! And with a website in both English and Turkish, no less. But I really don't recall ever—I'll have to check with Latty. She plans all my itineraries down to the last detail, even restaurants. She'd know—"

"You sure you want to freak her out with all this?" Dex asked, alarmed.

"Upon reflection," Milton replied, smiling but serious, "not on your life."

"Does the website have a phone number?" Dex asked, allowing a small sigh.

"He's got an e-mail address. Here, I'll open an e-mail to him. There. We can send a note. Why don't you come around and—"

Again, the panic.

"*Hellooo* in there!"

A lanky woman stepped into the room, rescuing Dex. She was so tall, thin and full of awkward angles, that all Dex could think of when he saw her were those hanging projects kids make in elementary school out of linked-up coat hangers. She was blushing as she pushed her tiny glasses up her nose. It was Evelyn Idun, director of the Home.

After she'd arranged Milton's transfer from the hospital, she'd made sure he got a room near her desk in the lobby so she wouldn't have to go far to check on him. When Dex had pushed his father's wheelchair into the building that morning, she'd made a big fuss and promised the twins she'd have him back on his feet in no time.

"Hello there, Evelyn," Milton said, offering a genuine but hesitant smile.

"You look fantastic!" Evelyn marched right to Milton's bedside. "The color has come back to your face." She put the back of her long-fingered hand on his forehead. Milton blinked, looking slightly overwhelmed.

"Amazing!" Evelyn said, "though I don't like the sound of that voice. Let's do some walking, shall we? You can do it. Two minutes, I promise."

Milton looked unsure.

"Go ahead, Dad," Dex urged. "Maybe I'll email the guy while you're out."

"Very well, then," said Milton, as if he had a choice. Evelyn was already hauling him out of bed and getting him situated behind his rolling walker. As they inched to the door, she complained that he never returned her calls. Milton said something about the messages probably getting lost on Latty's desk, but then they were gone.

The screen saver came up on the laptop, attracting Dex's attention. After a big sigh, he sat on the bed and touched a key, bringing up the e-mail form his father had opened. It was perfect the way things were working out. Perfect, except for the fact that Dex couldn't type.

As part of his lifelong campaign to camouflage his reading problem, he'd kept away from computers. When he had no choice, he'd sit and click away, pretending to know what he was doing, then stop and quit if anyone came to see what he was up to. Teachers assumed he was messing around with the computer's hard drive or visiting forbidden sites on the Web, and that was fine by him because it often got him kicked off.

But Dex wasn't going to lose this opportunity. He was going to figure out what this "dream" meant. If it were true, it was hard to believe. How in the world could his father wander into a random coffee house in Turkey and have some old geezer force a book on him that people had been chasing for millennia, only to wind up bringing it to another old geezer in Portland, Oregon, who wanted it to enslave the world? The coincidence was too much. He'd have to be some kind of—puppet.

Of course! Dex thought, jolted. He *was* a puppet! He wasn't controlling his thoughts and actions! Someone else was—and there was no doubt in Dexter's mind that this someone was Adem Tarik. Part of his dad knew it, Dex realized, and that's why he'd been saying he wasn't a bad man!

Dex concentrated on the screen, but almost instantly, the usual, crippling stress arose. It brought an acrid taste to his tongue and made him sweat. He glanced down at the keyboard, but the letters seemed to sway and blend, and now the screen shimmied in his vision.

Dex looked away, defeated that quickly. Furious, though not surprised, he pounded out some random letters and watched the meaningless symbols squirm across the screen. He could make out the large icon with an envelope halfway into a mailbox. *Screw it,* Dex fumed. He clicked it, sending off his jumbled letter.

"Dex!" someone called. It was Daphna, slipping into the room wearing a backpack and a strange, flushed look on her face.

Dexter jumped off the bed. His sister had obviously gone home to shower and change, which irritated him, but even so, he'd never been so happy to see her in his life. "What happened?" he asked. "Did you find him? Did you get the books?"

"Coming through!" Evelyn appeared in the door at that moment, just ahead of Milton. "Daphna, darling!" she cried. Dex knew Evelyn thought Daphna was the world's greatest kid for reading to the old folks.

"Hi, Evelyn," Daphna said.

Evelyn grinned, but then turned back to her charge. "Let's get you back into bed," she said, walking Milton slowly across the room. Halfway there, she looked at the twins and said, "Your father's doing super! Far better than I expected at this point."

Dex and Daphna smiled at this news.

"I'd love to stay and chat," Evelyn told them when Milton was comfortable again, "but I've got to go deal with the police. I still can't believe what happened! You two must be devastated. I know I said it before but, Daphna, your entire group murdered in cold blood!" Daphna nodded and looked away. She was devastated, even if she didn't have two seconds to notice it.

"Anyway," Evelyn continued, "I shudder to think what

kind of mess the police made of the Records Room. This is all too bizarre and awful if you ask me. That Mrs. Scharlach! She seemed like such a nice old lady!" Evelyn offered a sympathetic smile and then left the room shaking her head.

The moment she'd gone, Dexter bugged his eyes at Daphna to let her know he wanted the news. She bugged her eyes back as she took the pack off her shoulder.

"Dad," Daphna said, "remember that book we were telling you about, the really messed up one that makes no sense? The one you gave away? Well, I just happened to find it. Here it is." Daphna pulled the Book of Nonsense out and handed it to her father. Dex looked on, amazed by his sister's ability to get things done.

Blinking, Milton took the book and carefully examined its burned and gashed cover. "You know what?" he said. "This looks like a book I picked up for your birthday, kids. Did you find it in the house?"

"Um, yeah, Dad," Daphna said. "It was under your bed. I was vacuuming. I'm sorry if I ruined the surprise. Why did you get us such a crazy book?"

"No reason," said Milton, though he looked rather unconvinced. "Just a curiosity. I seem to have ruined books on my mind—"

"Thanks, Dad," Daphna sighed, taking the book back and trying not to sound disgusted. But it didn't matter. Milton had drifted off to sleep.

Dex waited a moment, then turned to his sister and asked, "Did you get the Ledger too?"

Daphna didn't respond at first. She seemed interested in something on the floor. Then she looked up, though not at Dex, and said, "No. Emmet told me he destroyed it. He died."

"He *died*? That's incredible! I don't know how you do it!"

Daphna's face dimmed.

Taking no notice of his sister's shifting mood, Dex shared what he'd learned: their father's "dream," and his theory that Adem Tarik was somehow still involved in all this, somehow controlling Milton.

Daphna lit up again. "Dex!" she said, "Emmet told me that Rash ranted about Adem Tarik every day, about what a loser he was for wanting to create Heaven on Earth."

Now it was Dex who lit up.

"What?" Daphna asked.

"Daphna, *Heaven on Earth*. When have we heard that

before?"

Daphna screwed up her face trying to remember.

"Someone found the Book of Nonsense after it was originally lost—"

"I know that, Dex."

"And that someone tried to train a group of thirty-six child geniuses to use the language—"

"I know that!"

"—tried to train them to bring peace to the world. *To make Heaven on Earth.*"

"He was the Benefactor!" Daphna cried, finally getting it. "He recruited the thirty-six kids to learn the First Tongue!"

"But why would he call Mom and send her into those caves?" Dex wondered, satisfied that they were on to the truth. "It was his book. Why wouldn't he get it himself if he knew where it was?"

"I don't know," Daphna replied. "Maybe it was too risky. But don't you see, that does explain why Mom would have gone on such a dangerous trip after she'd quit the search! Even if she'd already sold the store!"

"Yes," Dexter agreed. "She would've thought the search might end once and for all. Did Emmet tell you anything else about Adem Tarik?"

"No, nothing," Daphna admitted. "We've got nothing to go on."

"Not completely nothing," Dex said. He'd forgotten to mention that Milton had found a website for the coffee shop he'd dreamed about. "I sent this Fikret guy an e-mail," Dex said after explaining. "But it made no sense. I was mad and just pounded on the keys. You could write, though, and ask him about Dad's visit."

"That's great," Daphna said, brightening up further. "I'll do that later tonight."

Milton stirred in his bed just then. "Not a bad man," he muttered. "Adem Tarik—l—l—"

The twins waited him out, and when he seemed done, Dex said, "Okay, but there's something we'd better do a.s.a.p."

"What's that?"

"We need to destroy that book. Finish the job for the Council once and for all."

Daphna hesitated. "Are you sure, Dex?" she asked, surprising him. "I've been thinking. I know people abused the First Tongue when they knew it way back when, but does that mean people would abuse it today? Aren't we much more civilized now? Think of the power, Dex. Think of all the problems that could be solved if trustworthy people learn it. And we can be the ones to bring it back! If I learn it, I could teach it to you."

Dex was impressed by Daphna's passion, but any second thoughts she might have stirred just got wiped out. He'd been feeling a lot less angry at her since he spilled the beans about not being able to read, but the thought of her, already miss overachiever of the universe, teaching him like a toddler— well, that just wasn't going to happen, not in this lifetime. Dex was sure he'd never be able to pronounce the words right, anyway.

"No," he insisted, "don't you think the Council considered that? If they didn't want it around when they were the only ones who knew it, it must be bad news. People aren't meant to have that kind of power. *Any* people. Freaks like Picker would be bound to get a hold of it! We should burn it."

"I don't know," Daphna replied. A pained look crossed her face. "I don't think I could do it."

The thought of burning a book, rare or not, magical or mystical or otherwise, didn't faze Dex. But he knew Daphna could barely stomach seeing a dog-eared page in a worn-out paperback she didn't even like. "Daphna," he persisted, "Mrs. Tapi was trying to burn the book when Emmet got her, remember? That's what the Council wanted. For crying out loud, you're standing there holding a book that supposedly belonged to *God*. Do you think you're meant to drag it around like some overdue library book?"

"You're right," Daphna conceded. "You're right." Then she looked down at the book in her hands. "By the way," she said, "the pages are all changing. They're blurry. At least they were. Maybe they stopped, or maybe Dad's just too whacked out to know the difference. I almost puked looking at them."

"So?"

"So, I was wondering if this is what it looks like to you when you read regular books." Daphna held the book out for Dex, who took it with mild curiosity. He opened to the middle somewhere and looked down at a page. Immediately, his eyes dilated into two spotted green moons.

He could read the words on that page.

Dex snapped the book shut.

Daphna was genuinely hoping to get some insight into

what Dex had to deal with, but he was staring down at the book's tattered cover, his mind apparently somewhere else.

"Am I right?" she asked. "Are they moving again?"

"Yeah," Dex muttered, not lifting his eyes from the book.

Daphna looked at her brother. His cheeks, crimson when she'd come in, had gone a deeper red, and he looked almost clammy. "Are you okay?" she asked.

"That's—that's exactly it," Dex explained, massaging his forehead now. After a moment, he looked up, though there was no focus to his vision. "Only—it's a lot worse," he added. "I feel kinda sick now."

"Sorry," said Daphna, taking the book back, "it did the same thing to me. So, when do you want to do it?"

"What?"

"Burn it. If we do it here, we'll probably set off the alarm and Evelyn will have pandemonium on her hands again."

"Speaking of Evelyn," Dex said, regaining his focus, "I just got an idea. She said something about a Records Room, right? Maybe we can get in there and read up on all those old people in your group. They were all taught by Adem Tarik, right? Maybe we can find some clues."

"Great idea!"

Dex had to force himself not to look pleased.

"But," Daphna said, "let's go and do our own things for a while." Dex looked skeptical, so she explained. "Look, first of all I'm starving. And, anyway, if we suddenly seem like we're best friends, Latty's eventually going to think something's up. I know, we'll tell Latty we want to stay overnight with Dad. They have cots here. On the way over, we'll burn the book. Then, when everyone's asleep, we'll break into the Records Room. All the night nurses are on the second floor."

"Okay," Dex agreed, but then, with a trace of challenge in his voice, he said, "How 'bout I hold onto the book until then—so you won't get too attached."

After only a moment's hesitation, Daphna said, "I suppose that's reasonable." She handed the book over.

Dex received it with no small measure of surprise. He felt guilty for the surge of suspicion he'd felt, but even guiltier about what he was planning to do. He considered the incredible, fragile old book for a few seconds, then turned and left the room, too swept away by the shock at having been able to read The Book of Nonsense to think of saying good-bye.

Daphna, distracted by her own considerations, thought

nothing of her brother's hasty departure. In fact, she was pleased to have a chance to make sure the Ledger was still secure in her bag. She felt sorry for lying. She hadn't planned to do it, just like she hadn't planned to flirt with Emmet or use that Word to choke Wren and Teal. It all just happened. Things were just happening, and the best she could do was react.

The point is, Daphna told herself as she re-zipped her bag, *there's no use worrying about it. In fact, if Emmet's right, there's no use worrying about anything.* If events repeated themselves ten trillion times, she was just doing whatever she happened to be doing this time around. It seemed like the only rational thing to do was just to go with the flow. Besides, if she told Dex the truth now, he'd stop trusting her altogether. There'd be a screaming match, for sure. And what was the point of inviting trouble before it was due?

CHAPTER EIGHT
Burning Desires (Part i)

Everything went according to plan. Latty, who'd seen the news about a "bizarre incident" at the dump, was reluctant to let the kids leave after dinner, but she was touched that they wanted to stay by Milton's side.

After what appeared to be a rather tormented internal debate, she sent them off with a container of *Min-hun-t'ang* soup and several pleas to do anything and everything they could to make sure their father didn't think about what happened in those caves.

"And don't worry!" Daphna teased, putting her backpack over a shoulder at the door. "We'll protect him from that woman!"

Latty smiled, accepting the gibe, and waved her off.

Daphna turned to leave and saw Dex already hurrying down the road. He had his backpack over a shoulder and was carrying a large tin can. She rushed after him as best she could with the soup.

"Slow down, Dex!" Daphna hollered as her brother turned into an alley up ahead. When she rounded the corner, she saw him at the far end, stooping over the can, which he'd set on the ground. "I said wait up, Dexter!" Daphna protested, reaching him just as he lit a match and dropped it into the can. Instantly, multi-colored flames leapt up. Daphna jumped back. "What's going on? Why's it burning like that?"

"Lighter fluid," Dex answered. "I'm sorry I didn't wait, Daphna, but I had this huge feeling you were going to try to talk me out of it." Daphna looked cross, so Dexter added, "You're good at that. I didn't want to give you the chance," which took the teeth out of her glare. Brother and sister watched the flames transform the book into a pile of layered black tissue. It didn't take long, but to Dex it felt like forever because he was sure at any second his detail-oriented sister would realize that the book in that can was not The Book of Nonsense.

"So it's done," said Daphna when the last glowing red

sliver faded to gray.

"Finally," Dex sighed, watching her fearfully for signs of suspicion. He saw none.

There was a dumpster in the alley, so the second the can was cool enough to touch, Dex tossed the whole thing in.

"It sort of feels anticlimactic, though, doesn't it?" Daphna asked when it thunked inside.

"What do you mean?"

"I mean, it all seems too easy. We got the book and burned it. After all the Council went through—and for so long. It feels weird."

"We went through a lot too, Daphna. I don't how you can say it was easy. We were almost killed, like, two hundred times."

"I know. Believe me, I know. I just meant it seemed too easy to destroy. I mean, doesn't it blow you away to think that book might really have belonged to God?"

"Yeah. I guess," said Dex.

"You guess?"

Dex ignored his sister's tone. He'd never thought seriously about the idea of God. The few times he'd tried, it felt not unlike looking at the pages of a book—dizzying and pointless. Anyway, this was hardly the moment to start contemplating the subject again. "So, what have you been doing all day?" he asked.

Daphna considered pressing her point. It seemed important that Dex understand the incredible significance of what they'd just done. But then she thought, *Why?* He either appreciated it or he didn't.

Once again trying to avoid thinking the worst about her brother, it occurred to Daphna that though he'd been totally absorbed in their mission to pry the secrets out of that book, he hadn't expressed much fascination with the book itself. And why would he if he couldn't read it? A book that belonged to God would be nothing but the ultimate cruel joke to him.

"I just kind of hung out in my room," Daphna said, attempting to sound warmer. "I really needed some time to think about everything that's happened. I wanted to think about the Dwarves. It's all been too much. We've seen people die, Dexter. The whole world seems like it flipped upside down since we turned thirteen." This wasn't a lie. It's just that the list was incomplete. Daphna chose not to mention what she'd spent *most* of her time doing: scouring Rash's Ledger for other Words she could wield. And that she'd found one. "What did you do?"

"Oh, I just hung out in my room, too," Dex said, "with an ice pack." Like his sister had, Dex chose to leave out the most important details, which were that while using the ice pack all that time, he'd read the Book of Nonsense, scanning it for Words of Power. And that he'd found one. "My face is still killing me," he added. "Of course yours is killing me worse."

"Ha ha. Never heard that one before."

"Let's go," Dex said with a renewed sense of urgency. "We've got to figure out a way to break into that Records Room."

Daphna smiled, wryly. "Oh, that," she said. "I'm not worried about that at all."

"Why not?"

Daphna smiled again. "Trust me," she said, then walked swiftly out of the alley.

This time Dex had to hurry to catch up to her.

***

"Daphna!"

Someone had dashed out of a restaurant as the twins hurried by. *"Daphna!"* she called again.

The twins stopped and turned.

Daphna saw who it was and couldn't speak.

"Hey, Wren," said Dex.

"Ah, hi," Wren replied, giving him a dismissive once-over. Dex knew she hadn't the slightest idea who he was. "Anyway," she said, turning away from him, "Daphna, I'm glad I ran into you. How are you?"

"Um, I'm—I'm good. Thanks," Daphna stuttered. "We're kind of in a hurry, though."

"That's cool," Wren said. "I just wanted to let you know I'm having a party next Sunday night. A week from today. Just for fun you know, the last hurrah and all that before school starts. Just us girls. I'd love you to come. Around seven?"

Since he was basically invisible to her, Dex watched Wren closely as she spoke. Something was clearly not right. Aside from the obvious, that his sister was being invited to a Pop party, there was something about the indifferent tone Wren was affecting. It was covering something up. Something—he didn't know the word—predatory? It was there in her cool expression as well. But that's how Pops always seemed. Maybe it was just that he'd never gotten this close to one before.

Daphna didn't seem able to hold up her end of the conversation. She was probably speechless now that her fondest dream was actually coming true.

"She'd love to," he said for her, but not without bitterness. Why did everyone have to keep mentioning that school was starting up again?

"Great!" Wren chirped, though she gave Dex a look that made him feel like he was a repellent species with which she was only passingly familiar. "By the way, cute bag!" she added, then disappeared back into the restaurant.

The twins looked through the front window and saw Teal at a table with some other Pops. She smiled and waved, though her smile looked oddly anxious to Dex.

Daphna hurried down the road, so Dex had to catch up again.

"What was that all about?" he asked, coming alongside. "Did I just see what I think I saw? Did she really just invite you to a party? I thought you had to be a Pop to go to a Pop party."

Daphna shrugged, looking both pleased and somehow guilty, like she'd just been caught cheating or something. "You heard her," she said.

"But you're not a Pop." Dex scrutinized his sister. She certainly didn't look like her dreams had just come true. On the other hand, she had a bit of a smirk she was trying to hide. "I don't get it."

Daphna turned a sharp eye on her brother, but then collected herself. "I ran into her," she said, coolly. "Turns out they did lie about going to camp, but they apologized. So we're cool. Now let's get a move on or we'll—Oh, *gosh*—"

They'd reached the burned-out hulk of the ABC. The twins stopped and stood there gaping at the collapsed front room. A line of yellow tape strung around rubber poles cordoned off what used to be the entrance. The place looked desolate.

"Wow," said Dex. "Creepy."

"Hey! It's them!" someone shouted. The twins tensed. Six boys stepped out from behind the far side of the building.

"Run, Daphna!" Dex yelled, dropping his bag.

Daphna was too stunned to react. Dex grabbed her by the arm, causing her to drop both her bag and the soup, and tried to pull her away. But because they both reached back for their bags, the twins wound up in a tangled clutch, and then it was too late. The boys dragged them toward the steps leading down behind the warehouse.

Rough hands pushed and pulled them down the stairs and then shoved them up against the blackened rear wall of the building. Dirty fingers jammed over their mouths.

"Well, well, well, well, well," sneered a gangling boy with ferocious red hair. He looked back over his shoulder twice as he spoke, though no one was there.

Dexter recognized this hooligan. He'd been there in the park with his gang when Emmet made Dex piss himself. Emmet had shouted at him to keep away. Dex was scared, there was no doubt about it, but something deep inside whispered that this might just be a chance to redeem himself.

Daphna was terrified, plain and simple.

She had no idea who these boys were. Some of them looked like the kids at school who were always getting suspended, but she never went anywhere near any of them.

"You got a strange name," the redhead said to the twins. "Wax. What's up with that? Are you made of wax or something? If you caught on fire, would you melt?"

Dex and Daphna tried to look at each other to gauge the seriousness of this threat. For their efforts, they got their skulls slammed into the wall. The redhead took a lighter out of his jeans pocket and flicked it. A tall blue flame jutted out like a blade.

"Go, Antin! Go, Antin!" sang the boy with his disgusting hand on Daphna's mouth.

"Shut up," Antin barked. Then he said, "We've become very interested in fire lately." He stepped forward and waved the flame in Dex's face, revealing his herky-jerky black pupils. "Do you have any idea why we might be so interested in fire lately?"

Dex and Daphna managed to shake their heads.

"Tell 'em," the same other boy urged.

"Shut up. I'll tell you why," Antin said, stepping toward Daphna now with the flame. She recoiled from the blood-thirsty look in his eyes. "For one thing," he said, "this old place just went up. Very interesting, fires. They can really mess you up. You ever see how much a fire can mess a person up?"

Daphna had no idea how to respond to this. She was too frightened even to speculate about what was going on.

Antin didn't seem interested in her answer, anyway. He snapped the lighter shut and dropped it back into his pocket. "Funny you should ask," he said, looking over his shoulder.

"Here, I'll show you."

At his command, a boy with tattoos on his hands pulled aside a large piece of plywood resting against the wall, exposing a hole. Other boys pushed the twins through, then closed the hole behind them like the door to a dungeon.

It wasn't completely dark inside. They were in some sort of basement or lower storage area. Portions of the warehouse's floor above had collapsed, so the ground was strewn with debris that seemed to include charred books. A series of dim, flickering flashlights were set up in a half circle in the center of the space, projecting weak beams at something large and lumpy under a sheet. Little else was visible, making the object appear to float in an empty black sea.

"Over here," Antin ordered. He'd moved up ahead and was squatting down at one end of the thing. Then, for some reason, he suddenly swung his light toward the back of the storage area. He moved it around a moment, but quickly turned his attention back to whatever was on the floor.

When Dex and Daphna were pushed forward, he snatched the sheet away like a magician. But there were no flowers or birds or bunny rabbits in this trick. It was Emmet. Daphna looked down sadly at the body. The smell before was awful; now it was atrocious.

Dex was prepared for neither the sight nor the smell, and the shock, combined with the rank vapor he'd sucked into his throat, caused him to heave. The boys holding him leapt away, letting him to fall to a knee and vomit on the floor.

Everyone laughed.

So this was his redemption.

"We found him," Antin said, hauling Dex to his feet.

"So?" said Daphna, trying to gather her thoughts. But she was terrified, and horrified—and it was all too much.

"Sooo," Antin said, turning to Daphna with mock patience, "we want the scoop." He shone the flashlight at the body again. "What do you two know about good ol' Emmet here getting toasted?"

"Nothing," Dex swore. "We don't know anything about it."

"Don't be stupid, even if you are the stupid one," Antin spat, looking back and aiming his light in Dexter's face. "We found him in your little hideout."

Dex must have looked dismayed, because Antin laughed. "The other day," he explained, "after you and him put on that little show in the park, we saw him follow you into the woods. So I did a little following myself. He watched you crying like a sissy for a long time before he took off." Antin turned to Daphna then and said, "We found Mr. Well Done here right before he croaked."

Now it was Daphna's turn to look dismayed. She must have been wrong about Emmet being dead! She'd walked away from him, and he wasn't dead. These boys, these sick boys, must have been the people she heard in the woods.

"And guess what his dying word was," Antin said, giving a wildly exaggerated sniffle.

"I—I don't know," Daphna whispered.

"Nope," Antin quipped. Then he choked up with phony emotion and said, "His last word was—it was—'Daphna.' Isn't that touching? Anyone have a snot rag? I may weep." Approving snickers met this remark.

Daphna dropped her head.

"So what's the story?" Antin asked, switching to another voice, this one gossipy. "You and Emmet have a little thing going, or what?"

"No!" Daphna cried, disgusted by the mere suggestion. But Antin had given her an idea. It worked once, so—"I only got to know Emmet so I could ask him to help me meet you," she said, shyly. She was *still* using the poor boy. "I'm always too scared when I see you around."

"Why's that?" Antin asked, suddenly interested.

"'Cause—'cause—" Daphna sputtered. Her insides felt like they were rebelling. She didn't think she could go through with it without throwing up like Dexter had. No more words would come out.

"Well?" Antin said, the edge creeping back into his voice. Now the light was directly in her face.

Next time, Daphna told herself. It was now her motto. "I just think you're kind of cute is all," she said.

CHAPTER NINE
Burning Desires (Part ii)

"Daphna!" Dex yelled in disbelief, but two boys grabbed him and twisted his arm behind his back so far he couldn't speak.

"Fellas, fellas!" Antin said, turning round. "Did you hear that? Daphna here's got the hots for me!" He turned back to Daphna and said, "You're one of those good girls who go for bad boys, is that it?"

All the boys in the room laughed. Malevolent cackles in the dimly blinking dark.

"Why don't we go outside and talk about it," Daphna asked. She couldn't tell if she had the upper hand. It didn't feel like it had with Emmet. Not at all.

"Sure," Antin said. "Noooo problem." But he didn't move.

Daphna was rapidly losing her nerve. "Can we go now?" she asked.

Antin chuckled. "Sorry, Babe, business before pleasure. That's what I call my girlfriends—'Babe'—hope you don't mind. So, how 'bout you just tell me what old Emmet here was looking for."

"I told you," Daphna replied. "We have no idea."

"That's right," Antin said, "you did say that." He took a few steps toward Daphna, and the next thing she knew a vicious slap snapped her head to the side and sent her sprawling. She never saw it coming. The boys holding Dex clenched him even harder, but he didn't try to move. He could see his sister's silhouette crumpled on the ground, but he could not react to it. He couldn't feel anything because his mind was spinning away.

"Oh, I guess I shoulda told you," Antin said, helping Daphna, stunned and disoriented, to her feet. "That's what I do when my girlfriends lie to me."

Antin walked over to Dex and put his arm around his shoulder like they were best buds. "Chicks," he said. "Can't do anything with them, right? 'Specially the good-lookin' ones. So, what's the story, man?"

"We don't know any story," Dex insisted when someone took a hand off of his mouth. His arms were going to break if they didn't let up.

"I'll tell you a story then," Antin said. "When that freak-show showed up and started scaring kids off the streets around here, he was messing with our territory. We went to take care of him, but he told us he and the old man were up to something major. He said he'd cut us in on the deal if we backed off in the neighborhood for a while."

When neither Dex nor Daphna responded to this, Antin continued. "Soooo," he said, "when we found him all extra crispy-like in the woods, we tried to beat the story out of him for a while. But the big idiot wouldn't spill the beans no matter what we did—too stupid to feel pain, I guess."

The twins remained silent.

"Sooo," Antin went on, "old Antiny here had to do some figuring on his own, and this is how he figured it: Emmet here's burnt up, right? Good. And this place burned, right? Good connection, right? Solid. And that freak wrings your neck," he said to Dex. "You with me? And he croaks out your name before going kaput," he told Daphna. "Any of this making sense? Oh, wait, your old man sells books, right? Found that out too. And that old books can be worth a lot of money. You following me? Been all kinds of vultures around here sneaking off with burnt books. How this crap could be worth anything is beyond me. Lookit—" Antin bent down and picked up a book and opened it. It was too dark to see what it looked like, but it seemed heavy. "Just names," he said. "Like a gazillion names on every single page. Most of the books down here are just as stupid." He tossed it away. "Anyway," he said. "So what's the deal?"

"We told you—" Dex tried, but it was a feeble protest.

"Save it," Antin snapped. "We want to know what Emmet and the old dude were after. I knew you'd come snooping around here soon enough. So, unless one of you tells me exactly what I want to know, right now, we are gonna start melting some wax around—"

"How dare you!" Daphna suddenly screamed. Her cheek was still smarting, but her head was clear. She hadn't heard anything past the news that the gang had beaten Emmet. She leapt at Antin, already punching and kicking. She wanted to tear his hair. She wanted to scrape his eyes out for what he'd done to that lonely, dying, ruined boy.

Though she'd never physically attacked anyone before, all of the anger and frustration she'd been feeling about so many things burst out in a singular desire to hurt. Daphna wailed her arms and legs indiscriminately, trying to claw at the arms and hands struggling to get hold of her. Enough was enough. She was going to choke every last evil boy there with her Word—but now hands were on her mouth. She couldn't speak. She could barely breathe. Why hadn't she thought of that right away!

Antin started laughing again when Daphna was finally subdued. "I guess we know who wears the pants in the family," he sneered. "And speaking of pants, did your brother tell you what happened when old Emmet here—"

"He's gone!" someone shouted.

The boys who'd remained with Dex—none of whom heard him whisper a strange word the moment before they lost track of him—wheeled around to see where he was. But just then there was a violent whacking sound. Someone on the fringes of the group let out a whelp of pain and collapsed.

Moments later, there was a second smack, then another cry as a second boy fell. Bedlam ensued as everyone scrambled in a riot to get out. The blinking flashlights were kicked around in the mad rush and sent spinning in all directions like crazy, feeble searchlights. It was impossible to see where anything was. Cries followed one upon another as more boys crumpled in pain.

Daphna heard the repeated smacking and the heavy thumps of bodies hitting the floor around her, but she couldn't see what was making them fall. The lights were here, then there, whirling around. She caught a glimpse of one boy stagger as if he'd been hit in the back, but for the life of her couldn't see what hit him. Terrified, she crouched on the floor.

"Daphna!"

It was Dexter. He was somewhere nearby, but she couldn't see him. "What's going on, Dex? I'm scared!"

"Come on," Dex urged.

Daphna couldn't see where to go, but suddenly the board blocking the hole in the wall was pushed aside. She ran for it, getting only a brief glance back inside at the strewn bodies clutching heads, guts, and legs. Once out into the light, Daphna found her brother holding a broken piece of rafter. He tossed it aside, grabbed her by the arm, and pulled her back up to the street.

It was getting dark.

"My bag!" Daphna cried leaping to scoop it up. Dex grabbed his own, and the pair sprinted away. They ran full-out until they reached the R & R, but pulled up before going inside.

"How—when—I didn't know you could—what happened in there?" Daphna panted.

Dex, shaking and wheezing, said, "It was dark—they let go when you—I surprised them—" He met and held his sister's eyes, willing her to believe this unlikely story.

Daphna, also shaking uncontrollably, waited for more of an explanation, but none came. It was as if Dex thought it was no big deal to beat up half a dozen juvenile delinquents. Before she could ask anything further, he stepped around her and hurried into the lobby, so she followed, impressed with her brother like never before.

CHAPTER TEN
(Not) Breaking and Entering

After composing themselves as best they could, Dex and Daphna stepped into their father's room. They found him working on his laptop in bed. Daphna, trembling still as her adrenaline ebbed, noticed immediately he was typing much faster than usual.

"Isn't it amazing?" Milton whispered when she pointed it out. He apparently didn't want to strain his voice, which sounded like sandpaper now, but he flexed his fingers above the keyboard. "My arthritis isn't bothering me at all," he said. "It's been years since my hands felt so good. And my hip! It hurts so much less than—are you two okay? You're both pale. And Daphna, now *your* face is bruised. Did something happen? The two of you look like you've been through a war."

"Oh," said Dex, thinking his father had no idea how right he was. "We—raced," he lied, dropping his bag on the floor. "Daphna wiped out."

It was difficult to speak in a normal voice with his heart still throbbing. Dexter was on a high like he'd never experienced before. He could barely contain the urge to prance about and scream and pump his fists in the air. He'd just routed an entire gang. He, Dexter Wax, had just routed an entire gang. With every swing of that board he was taking out more than just those psychos. He was taking out the cruel kids in elementary school who challenged him to spell three letter words on the playground; he was taking out the domineering Pops in middle school who walked all over everyone; he was taking out every adult who'd ever lectured him about his lackadaisical attitude toward life and learning. This wasn't exactly the way he'd been hoping to start asserting himself, but it sure felt good.

Dex felt like some kind of superhero, and now maybe he'd have the confidence to find a way to feel like this all the time. He did wonder if maybe he'd used more force than was strictly necessary, but it wasn't like he hadn't been driven to it.

He'd figure it out later, when he had some time to think.

"I tripped on a curb," Daphna told their father. She put a hand to her cheek, feeling the pain now that the bruise had been pointed out. Then she suddenly realized they'd lost the soup. "Ah, I'm really sorry, Dad," she said, "but I kind of dropped the dinner Latty made for you, when I fell. It was your favorite again."

Milton offered a dismissive wave. "Don't worry about it," he said. "Evelyn brought me a great meal. She ordered out. Are you sure you're okay?"

"Sure, Dad. Are you getting sick?"

"Evelyn thinks I'm getting laryngitis, of all things. When it rains it pours, eh?"

"She likes you, huh?" Daphna walked over to one of the two cots Evelyn had brought in. She stashed her bag underneath one and then sat on her hands to make them stop shaking.

Milton blushed a bit, which was not something the twins had ever seen before. "Evelyn has never been anything but kind to me," he whispered, "though I'm afraid I've been too wrapped up in my business to appreciate it. Anyway," he said, changing the subject, "I'm really looking forward to this new trip to the Middle East. I've got a feeling I'm going to find something of great importance this time. But don't you guys worry, I'll be back before your birthday. I wouldn't miss your thirteenth for the world!"

Dex and Daphna flashed each other a vexed glance, but agreed to let this go. He'd said the very same thing before he left on the trip nearly two months ago.

"Oh, Dex," Milton added, "speaking of the Middle East, I got a very strange e-mail from that Turkish Coffee House owner you must have contacted, Fikret Cihan."

Daphna looked at Dex, perplexed.

"You did?" Dex asked.

"Yes, and he seemed extremely upset. What in the world did you write?"

"Nothing—I—What did it say?"

"He said your message—or my message, since it came from my account—was an intolerable insult. He said his grandfather is dead, but that it's all already on the way, though he didn't say what 'it' was. He said if I don't explain immediately, he'll come here personally to take it all back. Do you have any idea what he's talking about?"

"I have no idea," Dex replied.

"Did you ask him to send something?"

"Um, yeah," said Dex. It was easy enough to come up with a reasonable explanation for that. "I asked him to send me answers to the questions, for our assignment, I mean—and also, if he had any authentic items we could use for the presentation. Maybe he sent a bunch of stuff?"

"But he sounded so angry."

"Maybe my typing was bad or he took something I wrote the wrong way. Maybe his English isn't all that great."

"Well," said Milton, "I suppose anything is possible. Maybe I'll send him a quick note, just for clarification."

"I'll do it, Dad. Don't worry about it. It's probably my fault."

"All right," Milton said. "I am a bit tired." He apologized for being so tired all the time.

"That's okay, Dad," Daphna told him. "We're pretty tired, too." Milton seemed relieved to hear this, so the twins took turns in the bathroom getting into their pajamas, then turned off the light and climbed into their cots.

For a few minutes, they laid in the dark wondering how they'd know when their father fell asleep. But that turned out to be no problem at all because within five minutes, he was muttering, "Not a bad man—not—I—Adem Tarik—Adem Tarik."

The twins sat up when he stopped.

"When do you want to do it?" Dex whispered.

"We've got to wait until everyone's asleep," Daphna whispered back. *"I'm gonna stay up reading. It's been like, forever. I'll wake you up."* Then, with no further comment, Daphna curled into her sleeping bag. She switched a flashlight on inside and dove straight back into the Ledger.

Dex confirmed that his sister was safely cocooned, then slid deep into his own bag. He switched his light on and dove straight back into The Book of Nonsense.

"Dex!"

It was Daphna, whisper-shouting his name. Dex flipped his flashlight off and sat up out of his bag in a haze.

"It's 1:00 a.m.," Daphna said, noting how tired her brother looked. His hair was shooting out in even crazier directions than usual. She was tired too, of course, and was afraid to see what her hair looked like. "What were you doing in there? Sleeping with your light on?"

"Yeah," Dex said, blinking away the daze. "You look like

crap."

"Thank you so much. Let's go, already."

The twins sneaked out of the room and padded cautiously into the lobby. Some of the overhead lights were dimly lit, so it wasn't too difficult to see. Dex walked directly to the door behind Evelyn's desk, the one clearly labeled, "Records Room," and tried the knob. "Locked," he said, twisting it round. "Check the desk for keys."

Daphna, already standing next to the desk, tried the drawers, all of which were unlocked. She looked up, shaking her head.

Dex scanned the lobby for ideas. He looked up, remembering how he'd gotten into the ABC, and sure enough, another idea came to him. He walked over to Daphna and pointed up at the ceiling, which was made of square panels resting on thin metal strips. *Those lift right up,*" he whispered, "*same as in school. I might be able to crawl into a vent that leads in there.*"

Daphna thought this was a terrible idea. Dexter was going to get himself killed pulling a stunt like that. On second thought, it gave her a perfect opportunity.

"*Well,*" she whispered, "*go grab a flashlight. It's probably pitch black up there.*"

"*Right.*"

When Dex was gone, Daphna immediately focused all her attention on the Records Room door. Then she closed her eyes and thought about being behind it as intensely as she could. Slowly and clearly, she spoke the Word Emmet told her about, the one he'd used to get to the dump—the one, incredibly, that took her from her bedroom to her closet that afternoon. Twice.

Daphna felt nothing, but she opened her eyes and smiled. She was surrounded by tall gray filing cabinets in a dark and cramped little room. It worked again! It was incredible. She'd felt absolutely nothing, yet, there she was. But there wasn't time to dwell on it.

Daphna hurried to the door, opened it, and stepped back into the lobby. Dex was just coming back in with his flashlight.

"What? It was—How—?"

"*Shhh.* It was unlocked."

"But—I tried it!"

"*Shhh!* It sticks a bit. Come on already."

Dex looked at Daphna a moment and recalled how certain she'd been they'd get in. He tried to picture how well he'd worked the knob. The truth was, he was too groggy to remember. Maybe it was sticky. Dex slipped into the office behind his sister, slapping himself lightly on the cheeks.

Fortunately, the door had no window, so the twins were able to turn on the light and move around freely. The narrow little room was lined with cabinets, labeled alphabetically.

Daphna dove right into the Ws.

A familiar grunt of self-loathing burst out of Dex before he could stifle it. It was obvious he was going to be of no use, so he sat on the floor. He wished bashing things with heavy objects was necessary again.

Daphna looked up and saw the disgruntled look on her brother's face. She hurried her search through the drawer she'd opened and pulled a file free.

"Dad's," she said, holding it up, but Dex only shrugged. Daphna flipped through the sheets inside, but at the same time asked, "Do you have any idea what that guy, Cifan— whoever Cifan—would've sent Dad?"

"Fikret Cihan," Dex said. "And I have no idea."

"That's really weird. And you say you only typed a bunch of gibberish in the e-mail?"

"Yeah. Maybe he could tell I was pissed, or maybe I typed out, 'Your grandfather's a nut,' in Turkish or something."

"Why would his grandfather have the Book of Nonsense, anyway?" Daphna asked. "And why would he force it on Dad like that, just because he came in and asked about Adem Tarik?"

"Well," said Dex, "Adem Tarik must have given the book to him, and maybe he figured Dad was there to get it back for him."

"Yeah, that makes sense." Daphna put Milton's file back, disappointed that it had failed to explain pretty much anything.

"Nothing interesting?" Dex asked.

"It's all just medical forms from the hospital." She pulled the drawer out as far as it would go. "Hey," she said, "there's a huge book in the back here with some kind of straps on it." She reached for it, but noticed a second file with her father's name on it. It was the last one. "Look at this—" She lifted its contents out. "It's for Dad."

"A present?" Dex asked. Daphna was showing him a thin rectangular gift of some kind.

"It feels like a book," Daphna said, "but it's almost totally flat. Oh, that's weird—"

"What?"

"There's a tiny card attached that says, 'For my soul mate.' It's from Evelyn."

"Probably some book she thinks Dad wants," Dex said. "She was hitting on him when they met, on the plane ride we all took moving here. That's why Latty doesn't like her."

"Someone hitting on Dad," Daphna laughed. "That's about the biggest joke I've ever heard. And to still like him thirteen years later—that's kind of pathetic, actually."

"Yeah, it's like she's obsessed or some—Wait a minute!" Dex cried. "What if she's some kind of stalker? It's kind of a co-incidence that she happened to be on that flight from New York with us, isn't it? Maybe she's been following Dad!"

"What? *Shh!* I don't know, Dex. If you think about it, it's a coincidence that you meet anyone."

"But what if she really lived in Israel, and knew him there, and was in love with him, but he didn't know her—and then he married Mom. What if she was really jealous?"

"So she sent Mom away to get killed, and then followed Dad to Portland? Is that what you're saying?"

"Well, isn't that the kind of thing insanely jealous people do? I'll bet you Latty suspects as much, and that's why she's hated her all these years!"

"But," Daphna replied, "are you saying Evelyn Idun is Adem Tarik?"

"Maybe!"

"Dex, keep your voice down!" Daphna was skeptical. "Okay, let's say she's Adem Tarik, forgetting for a second that Ruby called their Benefactor a 'he.' I do remember that."

"So what! She also said the Council was called The Nine! She was a liar! And she also said she never actually met him!"

"True," Daphna conceded. "So let's say she wants to get Mom killed. Why? Let's say she's jealous and in love with Dad for some crazy reason. So she lures Mom into the caves and gets her killed. But Dad was there too. He could easily have been killed as well. He almost was."

"Us! That's why!" Dex said. "Maybe Mom and Dad were both supposed to be killed in the caves! Maybe she was going to try to adopt us or something!"

"Okay," Daphna pressed, "but how does that fit with being obsessed with Dad or calling him her soul mate all these years later? Wouldn't she have tried to kill him again in the last thirteen years?"

"Dad wasn't supposed to go to the caves," Dex declared, adjusting his theory. "She probably figured he'd stay home with us when Mom went for the book! She doesn't want to kill Dad, Daphna. She wants to marry him!"

Daphna had no reply to this. She had to think about it.

"We should at least try to find out if Evelyn ever lived in Israel," Dex urged. "We should go search her stuff."

"Dex, not everything is a crazy conspiracy, you know." Her own words rang a bit hollow to Daphna. The truth was, the world was turning out to be not just a book of secrets, but a library full.

"Let's open that gift!"

Daphna hesitated, doubting they'd be able to re-wrap it if it was nothing important. "Not yet," she decided. "Let's slow down, Dex. I have to admit your theory isn't totally un-reasonable, but it's only a theory, and it's only our *first* theory. It doesn't even begin to explain how she could have been the Council kids' original Benefactor. Let's do what we came in here to do. If we don't learn anything else, we'll tear apart everything Evelyn owns."

"Fine, whatever," Dex snapped. Daphna couldn't stand not being the one who figured everything out. The euphoria he'd felt after leaving the ABC had begun slipping away when he'd come into the Records Room. Now it was gone completely.

Daphna, disturbed by the totally unnecessary harshness in Dex's voice, slipped the gift back into its file and put the file away. Then she moved to another drawer while he glowered at the floor. It was strange. As long as Daphna could remember, her brother had been falling in and out of his sulky moods, but so much had happened in just the last few days that it seemed part of another time, another life even.

"Here's Mrs. Tapi's file," she said, pulling out another folder, hoping to move things along. "She's got a phony birth certificate here. I'll bet most of this stuff is phony. It must've been hard for them, having to reinvent themselves every generation. It says she was a librarian." Daphna knew she was talking to herself, but it helped her ignore the stifling atmosphere Dex was creating in the already stuffy little room.

"Here's something called an 'Intake Interview Report' from the home's psychologist," she said. "The rest home residents must have to do that." Daphna read it to herself as Dex watched with little enthusiasm.

"Not very interesting," she concluded. "Though it's kind of sad. It says when she was younger she lost a newborn baby and still seemed upset about it."

"Nothing about Adem Tarik, though?" Dex asked. "Like an address?"

"I wish," Daphna said, pleased Dex was at least paying attention.

"Here's Mr. Bergelmir's file." Daphna read through and put it back. "Nothing," was her conclusion again. "Just more fake background info. He was a bookbinder. Nothing interesting in the Intake Interview. Let me get Mr. Dwyfan." Daphna skimmed through the file, then put it back as well. "Nada," she moaned. "He was a publisher."

"That makes sense."

"What?" Daphna pulled out another file.

"They were all in jobs related to books."

"Right, of course. Hey, this is strange—"

"What?"

"I've got Mrs. Kunyan. In her interview she said the most difficult ordeal of her life was giving birth to a stillborn baby."

"What's strange about that?"

Daphna, her interest piqued, pulled out a thick file with Mrs. Deucalion's name on it and read through papers for a while. Despite himself, Dexter grew increasingly curious as she read. Finally, Daphna looked up at him and held out a blue sheet of paper. "Her medical report," she said. "Guess what."

Dex had no idea what she was talking about. "What?"

"Under 'Health Notes,' it says she suffered some internal damage due to a complicated miscarriage."

"And?"

"Don't you see, Dex? All three of the women on the Council lost babies."

"What does that mean?"

"I don't know," said Daphna, "but Mom was on the Council, and we didn't die."

"Wait a minute!" Dex cried, jumping to his feet. Maybe he had been too hasty condemning Evelyn.

"Shh! What?"

"I just remembered something Mrs. Tapi said in the park before Emmet got her!" Dex tried to keep his voice down, but it was difficult. "She said that when Mom told the Council she was quitting the search, they weren't surprised. She said—I remember her exact words—she said they weren't surprised because 'several of us did the same over the years, though our own tragedies brought each of us back.'"

"That's right!" Daphna cried. "They all left the search to have babies, even though they were all so old. But they all lost them—the tragedies—so they all went back. What does it mean? Why were they all trying to have babies?"

"I don't know," Dex said. "Didn't Mom say she just wanted a normal life in her note?"

"The note!" Daphna fumbled it out of her pocket once again. It was starting to tear.

CHAPTER ELEVEN
Family Matters

My Dearest Children,

I am writing to you now, just minutes before I leave on a most unexpected journey.

For so very long I have been searching for a book. This search has consumed my time in this world and denied me what I truly seek, what we all seek: to live, to love. May you never know loneliness like I have known. May you be surrounded by those who love you all the days of your lives. How blessed you are to have each other!

I broke my word, Children, and renounced the search. I found Love. Uttering those two small, simple words, "I do," set me free. And now I have you and my joy knows no bounds.

Only now it seems that the book may be within reach. I am going to find out. I expect the best, but something I cannot put my finger on worries me, and so I must write you this note. There is a man, Asterius Rash, who will go to any length to find this dangerous book, including murdering children. Should you ever cross his path, run! Under no circumstances should you have anything to do with this vile man.

It is my profound wish that you never read this note, for if you do, it will be because I am gone. I love you so much. I must admit I did not think it possible that you two could ever be. Two little miracles! Latona did me the greatest favor in my long life when she encouraged me to try for you. I need you both to

"STOP READING!" Dex ordered in a barely stifled scream.

"*What?*" Daphna cried. "We've got to be quiet! You scared me to death! What?"

"Daphna," Dex said, coolly, "what if it wasn't actually any of the women's ideas to have kids. Or, what if someone took advantage of the fact that they all wanted to and talked them into trying, someone who wanted them to have children for some reason. You just read the answer, Daphna.

'Latona did me the greatest favor in my long life when she encouraged me to try for you.' Dad told me the same thing earlier today!"

"Dex!" Daphna gasped. "How could you even suggest such a thing! Latty loves us. She's loved us for our entire lives!"

"I know," Dex admitted. "You're right. I know." He felt awful for even considering the possibility. "I'm such a jerk."

Dex waited for his sister to lay into him some more, but she didn't. She just stood there at her file drawer looking stricken.

"I'm sorry I said it, Daphna. Let's just move—"

"She is the one that took the phone call," Daphna said, her voice small and shaky. "What if there was no call?" She looked at Dex now with wide, terrified eyes.

"And she's the only one who had a story to tell about what happened in the caves," Dex put in.

"She can't be Adem Tarik, Dex. It's not possible. Is it?"

"Let's just pretend it is for a minute," Dex suggested. "Just to prove the theory wrong."

"Great! Good idea. Go ahead."

"Okay. Well, at some point she works her way into one of the female Councilor's lives. She sets them up with some man, then talks her into having a child, but the baby dies, so she moves on to the next one, and the next one, until she gets to Mom. Mom's kids are born okay, but just to make sure, she waits a few months—"

Daphna only looked more stricken at this. "This would explain why Dad went into a coffee shop when he doesn't even drink coffee," she said, looking horrified to say it. "Latty plans his itineraries."

Dex's emotions were jerked in another direction by this. If this were true, it was the explanation that kept eluding him, keeping a germ of doubt about his father festering.

The twins just looked at each other, sick to their stomachs not to have easily debunked this unacceptable theory.

"If Latty killed Mom," Dex said, speaking barely above a whisper now, "she probably tried to kill Dad, too."

"No," Daphna said, "not Dad. We'd've been sent away to some foster home or something. She would have needed him alive so she could move into our house. She would probably have knocked him over the head and pushed Mom over the edge before the collapse ever happened. Or, if she was really Adem Tarik, maybe she could have used the First Tongue to cause that collapse, or give Dad amnesia about it."

"Then when Dad got better, she kept him running all over the world on wild goose chases so he'd never meet a new wife who might not want her around—"

"Which would explain why she hates Evelyn," Daphna said, close to tears now. "And why she stayed at home and barely ever let us out of her sight." Daphna was reeling. "And why she's so freaked out about him remembering what happened in the caves! She's been waiting for us to turn thirteen, like everyone else! Dex, what are we going to do? I feel sick. I think I'm going to throw up."

"We've got to think this all the way through, Daphna," Dex insisted, trying to make up for starting this terrible train of thought. "None of this is actual proof. It's still just a good story right now. For example, if Latty sent Dad to Turkey for the Book of Nonsense, why didn't she get it from him right away when he got home?"

Daphna, nearly hyperventilating now, tried to get a grip on herself, but it was impossible with each plausible explanation that occurred to her. "Dad got in early!" she cried. "Latty was shopping, and I made him take me to the ABC the second he got out of his cab. He never even went in the house! Rash got the book from him right away. Remember how she about lost it when Dad mentioned Rash's name? She said it was just an awful name—She must've realized her plans had gotten screwed up!"

"Okay, but she didn't seem to want Dad to get it back."

"That's true!" Daphna agreed, seizing on this snag in the story like a lifeline. "In fact, I think she was avoiding Rash. I didn't really think about it at the time, but she didn't go into the ABC with Dad when they got there with that Latin book. With Dad halfway crazed, she said she was going to the toy store to buy us gifts!"

"She couldn't go in," Dex said. "I bet Rash met the Benefactor and she couldn't risk him recognizing her. Why else would she avoid him?"

"What does she want?" Daphna asked, or begged, really. "If she really is Adem Tarik, what was all that about making Heaven on Earth? And how does that make any sense if you go about it by murdering people? Maybe she gave that book to Rash way back when and told him to start the War of Words. Or, maybe she wanted the book to get back to Rash so he could try again."

The twins fell silent again, wishing they could go back to the state of ignorance they'd been blundering around in just minutes before. Some secrets were not worth knowing—they understood this now. They both felt as if they'd been pushed off a cliff.

Latty was the closest thing to a mother they had.

Finally, Daphna said, "We need proof. I refuse to believe one word of any of this without absolute, definite, irrefutable proof."

"No argument," Dex agreed. "But how do we get it?"

The twins considered the matter.

"We could spy on her," Dex suggested.

"We don't have time," Daphna said. "We have to force her to do something that makes it clear one way or another. I know, we can write her a note that shows we're onto her. If she's really Adem Tarik, we'll know by how she reacts. If she's not, we'll tell her it was some stupid sword and sorcery game thing of yours that wasn't meant for her."

"Tonight?" Dex asked, impressed with the idea.

"I could do it."

"But it's like, two in the morning or something."

"I need to know this is not true, Dex. And I need to as soon as humanly possible or I'm going to have a meltdown of monumental proportions. I'll make some noise that wakes her up so she'll see the note right away."

Dex could see his sister was serious, and after letting her deal with Emmet by herself, he felt he had no choice but to offer to go himself. It wouldn't be too difficult.

"I'll take care of it," Daphna said, not giving him the chance. She slipped past her brother and out of the room while he was still getting to his feet.

Dex reached the lobby only seconds after Daphna, but she was already gone. He looked around, confused. How could she have gotten out so quickly?

Dex paced to the entrance to see if she was just outside. It was too dark to see, but he did notice a little gray box on the wall next to the doors. It was a security panel with a blinking red light. The door was armed. Daphna must've headed for another exit. Dex chose the closest hall, his father's, and hustled down it, looking for another way out. The place was difficult to navigate because halls crisscrossed one another in irregular intervals. He hadn't ever spent much time on the first floor, not that it would've made much difference. Daphna could've gone any which way.

Eventually, Dex found another door, but it was armed, too, as was the third and fourth he happened upon. By that time, he was too frustrated to care where Daphna was. He didn't even know where he was. There were mounted signs of course, but they did him no good.

Dex raged up and down random halls, growing more and more aggravated until by sheer luck he found himself back in the lobby. After closing up the Records Room, he stalked back to his father's room, fed up again with just about everything.

CHAPTER TWELVE
Departures and Arrivals

Dex sat on his cot and sulked. But after what seemed like no more than fifteen minutes, Daphna walked back in. He'd wandered the halls for a while, but long enough for her to run home, sneak into the house, leave a note and run back? She didn't even look winded. *Not stinking likely,* Dex thought, but maybe she couldn't get out of the building. "Did you already—?"

"*Shhh!*" Daphna warned. "I went through the service doors downstairs—I sprinted! It's scary out there—I was afraid of running into those animals again." Noting her brother's disbelieving air, Daphna flushed with displeasure and said, "Do you want to know what happened or what?"

Dex did, so he pushed aside his growing suspicions for the moment.

"Well," Daphna whispered, "on my way over, I started thinking maybe the direct approach wasn't the best plan. I mean, I don't think Latty is Adem Tarik. I'm stating that for the record. But if she *was,* what do we think she'd do if we just came out and accused her of killing Mom? She'd deny it, obviously."

"So what did you write?"

"Well, first I wrote she shouldn't be alarmed that the note was delivered in the middle of the night. I said one of the nurses was getting off shift and lives right near us and didn't mind dropping it off."

"Okay. *So what did you write?*"

"I said we wanted to warn her about Dad before she came today."

"Warn her? About what?"

"Well, I said Dad's been talking more in his sleep and that he mumbled something like Mom didn't really slip off that ledge in the cave, that she was pushed. I wrote he sat up and yelled that she was murdered and then started saying he thinks he might know who Adem Tarik is. See, this way, if she was Adem Tarik, which she isn't, she'd think she hasn't quite been found out yet, but that she's going to be. I figure she'd have to do something right away."

"You mean like kill Dad?"

Daphna turned white.

"But she's not Adem Tarik," Dex assured her. "So she's not going to do anything, except maybe worry some more about Dad's nightmares."

"Right. Exactly. That."

"Did you put the note in the house?"

"I put it on the mat and made a lot of noise like by accident, then hid. When I saw the front light come on, I ran back. It all took, like, five minutes. She must've been up."

"Not bad," Dex said, but with little enthusiasm. It was a clever idea. He'd never have thought of all that. Daphna was up to something, he was sure of it, but he was too depressed and exhausted by the turn of events to care anymore. Dex climbed into his sleeping bag without offering his sister a goodnight.

Daphna climbed onto her bag as well, relieved not to be pressed any further about her trip home. She'd tried to wait a bit before teleporting back, to make it seem more believable, but she clearly hadn't waited long enough.

Both twins burrowed into their bags, so neither noticed the other's flashlight come on, nor did either comment when, ten minutes later, their father mumbled in what was now a Rash-like raspy voice, "Adem Tarik, Adem Tarik—I—am—I—not a bad man."

***

"Kids! Kids! Up and at 'em! Kids!"

Dex and Daphna both jerked to woozy attention and flipped their lights off. Neither had slept a wink.

"Rise and shine! *Hello?*" It was Milton, sounding like he was gargling steel wool.

Dex freed his head from his bag and blinked groggily at his wide-eyed father, sitting up in bed. A moment later, Daphna's head emerged. She had dark circles under her eyes.

"What gives?" Milton asked, noting the twins' equally bleary looks. "Are those cots that bad? I wanted to let you sleep, but it's already eleven, and I'm wondering where Latty is. She should've been here an hour ago, and there's no answer at home. I'm hoping one of you wouldn't mind running over to see what's what. I almost feel good enough to do it myself, but Evelyn would have my head if she knew I was even thinking about—"

"We'll both go!" they twins offered, already on their feet.

Daphna rushed into the bathroom before Milton could get another word out. He looked quizzically at Dex.

"I think she just really wants her own shower," Dex offered by way of explanation. "I just want some more sleep. The cot was a little lumpy." Dex noticed a tray of bagels and apples had appeared in the room. He grabbed one of each.

"I'm sorry about that, Dex. I could talk to Evelyn. But to tell you the truth, I don't think I'll be in here much longer."

"That's okay."

Daphna rushed back out just then, so Dex hurried into the bathroom behind her.

"Sorry to bolt out of here, Dad," Daphna said, grabbing her own bagel and apple.

"That's fine. I'm going to be doing some heavy-duty walking today."

Dex reappeared, so the twins put on their backpacks, said good-bye to their father, and hurried straight outside. They walked home eating ravenously, anxious and afraid to learn what Latty's absence meant. They agreed without agreeing not to talk about it on the way.

But the moment their house came into view, it was obvious something was amiss. Every light was on, and the front door was standing open. The car was also gone, which meant Latty was too.

The twins dashed inside ready for—they didn't know what they were ready for. What they found was about the only thing they hadn't expected: that is, nothing.

Nothing seemed wrong.

Dex and Daphna looked around the living room and then walked into the kitchen. They came back out, shrugging.

"Something's off," Daphna said. "I just can't figure out what."

"Yeah," Dex concurred. "It's different in here." The twins remained standing where they were, looking at everything as if for the first time.

"*What is it?*" whispered Daphna, turning about, scanning the bookshelves and coffee table and couch.

Dex was doing the same. He turned himself in a full circle before his eyes settled on the mantle above the fireplace.

"Look," he said, pointing to the blank space on the wall

above it.

"Mom's picture!" Daphna hurried over and put her hand on the wall. She had no idea what it meant that it was gone. It was strange not to have noticed it was gone right away.

Dex turned to look at the collection of small, framed photos on the shelves and coffee table.

They weren't there.

Daphna, certain what she'd find, rushed to the built-in cabinet below the shelves and threw open the doors. "All our photo albums!" she cried. "They're gone!"

Dex hurried into Milton's room and called out, "They're all gone in here too—even the giant one of Mom over his bed!"

Daphna noted the same in the kitchen and in the office. Then, at the same moment, the twins ran to Latty's room.

Empty.

It was deserted.

There was a stripped mattress, an empty closet, and barren dressers. It was as if it were an unused spare room.

The twins, stunned by the sight, backed into the living room and sat down on the couch. Whatever they thought the letter might make Latty do, this wasn't it.

Neither Dex nor Daphna spoke. Neither wanted to be the one to say the words. But the truth sat there in the room with them, stinking like rotting meat.

"I always forget people's exact words," Daphna finally said. "But I remember exactly what Ruby Scharlach told you when I was listening at her door at the R & R. She said that sometimes even those closest to you cannot be trusted." A bitter mini-laugh escaped Daphna as the irony of this remark hit home. She'd been lied to by the one person in her life she'd continually confided in, even if it had been a while since she and Latty had really talked. Not only had her supposed friends at school turned out to be frauds, her supposed best friend at home had too.

"Why'd she take the pictures?" Dex asked, staring dumbly at the front door, which was still ajar. He was so tired and beaten down that it came out as a whimper. "Why'd she have to do that? It's like she stole our past. Those pictures of Mom were all we had of her."

"She's evil," Daphna snarled, feeling prickles on the back of her neck. "She wanted to hurt us on her way out. We were right, Dex. We've been living with Adem Tarik for thirteen years! We've been living with the person who killed our mother our entire lives. She took Mom's body once, and now she's taken her memory!"

And that was it for Daphna. The floodgates opened, and she started to sob. Dexter sat next to her, still staring at the door, a zombie.

Daphna sobbed uncontrollably for ten minutes and showed no signs of slowing down until Dex said, "So, what are we going to do now?"

At this, Daphna suddenly stopped crying. She turned to her brother with swollen, red-rimmed eyes, looking surprised by the question. "We're going to find her," she said, sounding as if this was the most obvious thing in the world. "We're going to find her and make her pay."

This shook Dexter out of the shock he'd been in. He got up and paced around the living room. He'd never seen such a savage look on his sister's face before. He was angry too— hurt and angry—but she looked downright murderous. He did suppose Daphna was a lot closer to Latty than he was, though it didn't seem like it recently.

He had no idea what they should do now. What were they going to tell their father? Could they stall his coming home? Could they make a new effort to get him to remember everything so he'd understand, once and for all? Did they really want to make him remember seeing his wife get murdered?

Dex went to close the door, but before he got it shut, a long delivery truck pulled into their driveway. "Hey," he said, "what's this?"

Still raging, Daphna got up and hurried over.

The truck stopped alongside the house, and a muscular deliveryman hopped out with a clipboard in hand. He approached the twins, who'd come out on the porch, and asked if a Milton Wax lived there. A pin on his work shirt said 'Ireneo Funes.'

"Ah, yeah," said Dex. "But he's in the hospital."

Ireneo looked disappointed. "Either of you eighteen?" The twins shook their heads, but he looked like he knew they weren't anyway. "Anyone home who is?"

"No, but we can sign," Daphna offered.

"No can do. Could lose my job." Ireneo tore a card from a pad and handed it to Daphna. "Have your father give us a call to arrange another time for delivery."

"Really, we're very respons—" Daphna insisted, but Ireneo was already heading back to his truck.

"Do something, Dexter!" Daphna whispered. There was no possible way she was going to flirt with a grown man, but she was too worn out to think of anything else. "It's gotta be from that guy in Turkey! The stuff he said was on the way!"

Dexter hurried after Ireneo, who'd climbed back into his seat. Daphna heard him say something, then he came running by her and back into the house. "I'll be one second!" he shouted.

Daphna was pleasantly surprised at her brother's lack of hesitation and extremely curious to know what he was doing. She walked casually over to the far side of the truck to see if Ireneo might say anything to her, but she found him sitting in his seat, staring through the windshield with a dull, slightly misty look in his eyes. She cleared her throat, but he didn't respond. He had that expression some kids get in school when they're so bored they have no idea where they are anymore.

"Ah, sir?" Daphna tried, growing concerned. She was about to lean in to get a closer look at the deliveryman's eyes, but Dex called out from the house that he was coming. When he appeared at the driver's side door, Ireneo turned and blinked at him.

"I was hoping you could make an exception?" Dex said, holding out a bulging envelope.

"Huh? I've got to get go—"

"An exception," Dex repeated, putting the envelope into Ireneo's puzzled hands. "I'm sure they let you make exceptions sometimes. You know, about the age requirement."

Ireneo opened the envelope, but immediately squeezed it shut again. Daphna had seen enough to understand, a fat flash of green. Suddenly, Ireneo was climbing back out of the truck.

"You're right," he said, shoving the envelope into a long pocket on the side of his pants. He strode around behind the truck and the twins followed after. "They do make exceptions for minors, like, for times when the only adult is ill. You can go ahead and sign your father's name." Ireneo handed his clipboard to Dex, then began unlatching the cargo door.

"No problem," said Dex, scribbling away with relish. "We really appreciate—" Dex stopped short when the door rolled up. Both twins stared, transfixed, into the truck. Inside were boxes, hundreds and hundreds of boxes, all the size of milk crates, all with their father's name and address on them.

"Is this all for us?" Daphna asked.

Ireneo nodded and began pulling boxes out and setting them on the driveway.

"Can we see what's in them?" Dex asked.

Nodding again, Ireneo pulled a box cutter out of his back pocket and sliced open a box he'd set down. Then he went back to unloading.

The twins leapt to the box and pried up the flaps like it was the birthday gift they hadn't received.

Inside were thick bundles of low-quality paper tied up with string. Dex fell back as if he'd discovered his present was a wasp's nest. Daphna, on the other hand, was thoroughly intrigued. She pulled a bundle out, untied it, and fingered through some pages. Her eyes grew wide. After a while, she put the bundle back in and pulled out another, then two more.

"Are all the boxes full of the same thing?" she asked, turning to Ireneo. He shrugged and tossed her the cutter.

"What are they?" Dex asked.

"Hold on," Daphna replied, cutting open two other boxes. They were both filled with the same bundles. She pulled a few out and flipped through them, then put them back. "There must be thousands of these in that many boxes," she said, slightly awed.

"Yeah, but what are they, Daphna?"

"Sir," Daphna asked, "is this all from Turkey?"

Ireneo took the clipboard back from Dex, checked it over, and said, "Yeah, from a *Feekret Ceehan.*"

Daphna was enjoying keeping him in suspense, Dex could tell, and he decided to let her know what he thought about it. He turned to Ireneo and asked if he'd mind giving him a moment to talk with his sister in private. Ireneo had no problem with this. He stepped back around front and climbed inside the truck.

"Dex, how much money did you give him?"

"I don't know. I just grabbed a couple handfuls."

"But why was he just sitting there, all spaced out when you went inside?"

Dex sighed. "I have no idea."

"It was weird."

"Are you going to tell me what these stupid papers are or not!"

"Just lists of random words," Daphna said. "Bizarre ones. They're copies of the Book of Nonsense, Dexter. The old guy who gave Dad the Book—that's what he was doing when Dad came into that shop! He was copying it in case the First Tongue reappeared, and he had to keep copying because, for all he knew, it might appear only one Word of Power at a time."

Dex looked into the truck and said with wonder, "He must have been doing it for his entire life. I bet he had no idea what he was doing it for."

"But he sure knew *who* he was doing it for!" Daphna cried, "Adem Tarik! Who was busy trying to get Council members to have babies!"

"Dex," said Daphna. "Latty sent Dad to get the Book of Nonsense, but also to get all these papers. Maybe that explains why she didn't care about the actual book when Dad brought it back! She had to know everyone would come and start killing each other over it. It was a lure! What she really wanted were the copies!" Daphna's temper flared up wildly again. "I mean, there was no way the First Tongue was just going to happen to be in the original book just because we turned thirteen!"

Dex shrugged, as if not entirely convinced. Then he seemed to think of something. "But, that's strange," he said.

"What's strange?"

"Well, the only reason anyone would want the Book of Nonsense, or those copies, would be to learn the First Tongue, right? And that's strange because Adem Tarik should already know it, right? She wasn't part of the Council. She didn't make herself forget it like they did. She *found* the language in the first place. She could write her own book full of Words of Power if she wanted one."

"True," Daphna agreed. "I don't know what that means, and I'm way too tired to figure it out."

"Yeah, me—No, wait a minute. Remember what Ruby told us about how the kids had to learn the Words of Power?"

"No, Dex," Daphna sighed. "I really don't."

"She said they had to puzzle out the Words themselves."

"She can't do it!" Daphna cried. "Maybe her plan all along was to have the kids learn the language *so they could teach it to her*! Maybe she was blind, like Rash! Maybe that's what she wants with us!"

"That would make sense," Dex replied, "except for one small thing."

"What's that?"

"Latty isn't blind."

"Oh, right," Daphna said. "I told you I was too tired. I give up, Dex. I can't deal anymore."

"Me neither. And anyway, whatever the truth is, we better get busy."

"What do you mean?"

"By the looks of it, we're gonna be spending the next ten hours burning paper."

CHAPTER THIRTEEN
Fired Ideas

Dex had to bring out another envelope, but it wasn't too thick, and it helped Ireneo forget the deadlines that started worrying him again. It took nearly ninety minutes, but he and the twins managed to haul all the boxes into the living room. They were stacked everywhere. Awkward piles overwhelmed the couch, the chairs, the shelves, the coffee table, and the floor. The tallest stacks reached as high as the twins' shoulders.

When Ireneo finally left, Daphna called Milton. She told him Latty wasn't feeling well and that she and Dex were staying home with her. He said that was fine because he was going to see a bunch of doctors all day, anyway. Evelyn wanted them to confirm that he was recovering as fast as she thought he was. He said he might even try to talk them into sending him home in the morning if it went well.

As good as this news was, it made the twins frantic. They very briefly considered letting their father see all the bundles, thinking the incredible number of them alone might make their story more believable. But that was a long shot, and they quickly agreed it was more important to destroy any remaining source of Words of Power.

Though thoroughly exhausted, neither thought they could afford to rest at all. So, as soon as their minds were made up, the pair cleared a path through the boxes to the fireplace. Dex used one of the bundles from an opened box to get a fire started, and Daphna, sitting on the hearth, began feeding them in a few at a time once the flames took hold.

It was slow going, incinerating that much paper. The fireplace was only so large, and putting too many bundles in at once choked the flames. Also, scoops of ash had to be hauled out when it heaped up too high.

For a while, Dex tore out pages from the bundles for Daphna to throw in one at a time. They burned better, but it soon became obvious it would take days to do it all that way. The twins had no choice but to feed in the full bundles and wait.

Feed and wait and scoop. Feed and wait and scoop. Both were too tired to talk. After a while, the repetition and the quiet and the steady heat from the fire finally got to Daphna. Leaning against the side of the fireplace, she nodded off.

"Daphna!" said Dex, poking her in the leg with a bundle.

Daphna jolted awake and suddenly asked, "Did you tell that delivery guy what you were doing when you went into the house?" She'd been thinking about it as she fell asleep, about the way Ireneo said he was in a hurry, but then just sat there waiting like he hadn't a care in the world—like he was meditating or something.

"I don't know, Daphna. Just keep burning."

"You don't know? It was like, two hours ago."

"Look, Daphna, I'm too tired to remember insignificant details, okay? Just keep burning!"

"Do not yell at me, Dexter."

"Then stop interrogating me!"

"Interrogating you? Is there something I should be interrogating you about?"

"No."

"Maybe I should interrogate you," Daphna pressed. Now that Dex mentioned it, she would like some things explained. "How about I interrogate you about how you learned to beat up an entire gang when you've never been in a fight in your entire life."

Dex stood up and flung the bundle he'd been trying to hand Daphna into the fire. "How about I interrogate you!" he challenged, stepping toward his sister.

Daphna stood up and leveled a cool gaze at her brother. They were nearly nose to nose. Dexter wasn't going to get a rise out of her with the stupid new way he'd been looking at her when he got mad, or by crowding her either. "I told you not to yell at me," she said through clenched teeth. "And get out of my face."

Dex, realizing he was about to lose it, stepped away. "Fine," he snarled, "but how about you tell me something. How about you tell me how you really got that office door open. How about *that?* How about you tell me how you went home and wrote a note to Latty and then got back to Dad's room in, like, ten seconds flat."

Daphna cut her eyes at Dex, but she'd been put on the defensive. "I told you," she snapped, "the door was unlocked, and I ran."

"Right," Dex said. "Then why don't you just keep your questions to yourself, and I'll keep mine to myself."

"Fine."

"Fine."

Having reached this agreement, Dex went back to handing over bundles, which he did with overt hostility. Daphna snatched each one from him and jammed them into the fireplace as soon as there was room. When individual boxes were empty, Dex cut them up to be burned along with the pads.

The twins worked this way for several more hours, taking only a short break for sandwiches. Slowly, very slowly, the number of boxes began to dwindle. Not another word passed between them all the while.

Eventually, the twins' tempers fizzled. Both started thinking about Latty, and both had similar thoughts. They wondered what it meant that she was Adem Tarik, that they'd lived under the same roof with her, that she'd been, for all intents and purposes, their mother.

Daphna fumed about the betrayal. All she could think about was finding a way to lash out at Latty. *There can't be anything wrong with getting back at people who've intentionally hurt you,* she thought—*not if you're in the right, not if you want justice!* An image of Wren's and Teal's strangling blue faces floated across her mind's eye. It was all the convincing she needed. She'd learn to live with betrayal better next time.

Dex's primary feelings were confusion and dismay. He cast his mind back over life with Latty. Beyond her constant fussing, beyond her meddling in his and Daphna's every affair, the only thing he could see was what looked for all the world like genuine love and concern. As far as he could tell, she couldn't have cared for them more had they been her own flesh and blood.

How could the world be so phony? he wondered. His father, who'd always appeared to care little or nothing for them, was actually full of love—and now Latty turned out to be—what, he didn't know. But she killed their mother. What kind of world was it where no one was what they appeared to be? Dex had refused to give any real thought to the possibility that the book they'd found really belonged to God. But, now that he considered the matter, if God really did create the world, what was he thinking? Why would he make a place where people can murder your mother when she's only trying to do good? Why would he make a place where people can travel halfway around the globe to deceive you, hurt you, try to kill you—just because you were born to certain parents?

And, Dex thought, his confusion slowly transforming into dark resentment. *What kind of God makes a world where your life has to suck because you can't read because your eyes weren't wired to your brain right?*

Even these thoughts petered out for the twins, who finally let their minds go blank. It wasn't exactly sleep, but it helped. There was something mesmerizing about the repetitive work involved in all the burning, and the flicking tongues of fire devouring the pads were hypnotic too.

It took nearly six hours, but finally the last bundle burned. The twins looked at each other warily when they'd finished, exchanged grudging nods for their accomplishment, then grabbed their overnight bags and staggered toward their rooms. The sun was already starting to go down.

Daphna sank into her bed. She opened her bag, took out Asterius Rash's Ledger and put it on her lap. In her current state, it was nearly impossible to read, especially after having stayed up all night squinting at Emmet's weird writing in her sleeping bag, but she needed to learn as much as she could. Events were spiraling out of control, and the only thing comforting her now was the incredible potential of the Ledger.

So far, she'd only been able to make those two words work. She had to keep trying new ones. If she didn't come up with some more subtle skills, Dex was going to catch onto her, for sure. Daphna didn't feel badly about lying to her brother anymore, not with the way he'd been acting.

She opened the book and chose a Word at random. It took a moment to make it out, but when the letters finally came into focus, she said it out loud. It sounded Chinese. Nothing happened.

Daphna was about to try it again, but a crude voice outside her slightly open window distracted her. "Shut up!" it hissed.

Antin!

With energy she didn't think she still had, Daphna lunged to her light switch, flipped it off, then crawled on her hands and knees over to the window, still holding the Ledger.

Antin was outside, laying into one of his gang. "I'm not gonna tell you again," he warned, "the guy snuck up on us in the dark. He's a coward!"

It took a second for Daphna to realize he was talking about Dex.

"I'm telling you, Antin," a boy protested, "I was looking right at him when his sister went ape. And the next thing I knew, he was gone. Then I saw Poly go down. All of the sudden he was just lyin' there bleeding."

"Don't think I don't know what you're doing!" Antin railed. "You all panicked. You freaked. It's that simple. And the next time you hand me that load, you're the one who's gonna disappear. Got it? When the rest of those wimps get better, I'm gonna kill them. Now I'm telling you, we're gonna find out what the big mystery is all about right—"

Daphna didn't hear the end of Antin's rant.

With her face aflame, she got to her feet and stormed out of the room. The fact that Antin and who knew how many of his goons were about to invade her home was suddenly the furthest thing from her mind. Daphna was running by the time she reached the kitchen. She tore open the basement door and practically flew down the steps. Only a lucky grab at the banister halfway down saved her from winding up on her face at the bottom.

Dex, sitting at his desk, was too stunned by his sister's kamikaze attack on the stairwell to put the Book of Nonsense away. He'd been leaning over it, but was now looking wide-eyed at Daphna, who was draped over the railing, her face twitching with rage.

"I KNEW IT!" she screamed. "I KNEW IT! *That*'s why you ran ahead of me with that can. What an idiot I am! No wonder you soaked it in lighter fluid! Let's finish the job for the Council," she mocked. "We're the only ones left to do it, Daphna! You thought I'd talk you out of it, huh? YOU NEVER INTENDED TO DESTROY IT! As soon as you looked inside it in Dad's room!"

Daphna went suddenly silent. Dex hadn't said a word or moved a muscle.

"But," she said, losing steam and thoroughly confused, "you can't read. How—when you can't see the—Wait a minute! I showed you the book 'cause the words were changing. They were moving around. You can read it, can't you? The moving words look steady to you, don't they? You learned how to make yourself invisible, and that's how you beat up all those boys, and you learned a way to make the delivery man stay when you told him to!"

Dex smiled in a disturbingly satisfied way. He nodded.

Daphna's fury redoubled. "YOU'RE A LIAR!" she wailed. "YOU'RE A LIAR, DEXTER WAX!"

Dex still wouldn't speak, but his smirk was getting wider and wider by the second.

"What!" Daphna demanded. "Why are you looking at me like that?"

"Because you learned how to teleport, and that's how you got into that office, and that's how you got home to leave that note so quickly."

Daphna, poised to unleash an even more howling attack, went pale. "That's ridiculous," she snarled, but it was a lame protest. How could he know? "What are you, some kind of mind-reader now?"

Dex laughed. "No, I'm a palm reader."

Baffled, Daphna looked down at her hand. Which was still clutching the Ledger. She sighed, defeated and finally aware of what a massive hypocrite she was.

"Emmet destroyed it, eh?" Dex said. "I guess we're both idiots, huh?"

Brother and sister regarded one another cautiously now, unsure how to proceed. They were deadlocked. They'd both lied. They'd both acted selfishly, possibly jeopardizing everything they were trying to accomplish.

"Dex," Daphna said when the staring contest wore her down. It didn't take much. "I'm glad you know. I'm glad you did the same thing. I'm sorry, but—"

"But what?"

"I'm beginning to think it doesn't matter what we do, good or bad. In a way, it's like we have no choice, anyway."

"What?" That made no sense to Dexter, and he was far too sleep-deprived to puzzle it out.

"It's like Emmet said to me," Daphna explained, "if time is endless, we'll live a trillion times, and we'll do everything: good and bad and in-between. It doesn't really make a difference when we do which. It's like, if I make the right choice now, it just means I'll make the wrong one later. It's almost totally random. So, like I said, it's just the same as having no choice at all."

"That's a really touching apology, Daphna," Dex muttered, but his thoughts went immediately to his own insights. If that were true, and he'd understood correctly, he wouldn't have to worry about whether he'd gone too far with that board. "You don't need a trillion lives to see how random the world is," he said, "you only need one. Just look at us. One kid gets born with everything and the other one gets screw—"

A loud creak overhead made Dex look up at the ceiling. Daphna snapped her eyes up, too.

The floors creaked again.

"*Oh, no!*" Daphna whispered. They'd left the front door open to keep the living room from overheating from the fire. "It's Antin!" she mouthed. How could she possibly have forgotten?

Dex jumped to his feet. "Can you get these books out of here?"

Daphna nodded. "Good idea. I'll put them in Dad's room at the R & R," she said, then closed her eyes and uttered an odd sounding Word. Daphna opened them again, only to find she was still in the basement. She repeated the Word, but still nothing happened.

"What's going on?" Dex whispered. The sound of feet walking stealthily overhead was getting louder because more people were up there now.

"It's not working!" Daphna whined, nearly frenzied. "I'm too tired. I can't say it right!" She tried three more times, but each time the Word sounded different. "Let's hide under the stairs!" she whispered. There was a storage closet there with a door that you had to push to pop open. There was no knob, but it was still obviously a door.

"No," Dex said, trying to stay calm. He'd have to handle it again. And why not? It was easy last time. He'd be lying to himself if he didn't admit it was fun. Dex spoke the Word that made him invisible, then moved confidently toward the steps.

"*Dex*," Daphna hissed.

He turned. "What? I'll take care of them."

"I can see you."

"Ahhh, the Candle Twins!" cooed a syrupy voice from the top of the steps. "It's sooo nice to see you!" It was Antin. Three of his flunkies were standing behind him, all looking much less excited than their leader about the reunion. One had a black eye, and the other two had casts on their arms. Antin looked fine, though.

Dex backed carefully down the steps. He tried his Word again and looked at Daphna. She shook her head.

"Girls!" Antin snapped at his gang when they didn't immediately come down behind him.

They obeyed reluctantly, limping, until all four boys stood

facing the twins, who'd retreated to the rear of Dex's room. Dex and Daphna's obvious exhaustion and increasingly worried expressions must have been reassuring because the boys gradually took on their normal menacing scowls.

"Man," one of them said looking around, "get a load of this dump. This is worse than your place, Antiny. You were wrong. He ain't a chicken, he's a pig!"

Antin snorted, mildly amused.

Despite the gravity of the situation, Daphna looked around. It was true. There were piles of dirty clothes heaped across the floor along with a vast assortment of what could only be described as junk. It looked like Dex had taken apart everything in his room that could be taken apart and then scattered the guts around like seed on a lawn.

"I told you it was a total fluke what happened," Antin said. "But you ain't seen nothin' yet." He plunged his hand into his pocket. The twins both feared the lighter, but this time Antin produced a knife. Expertly, he flipped it around in his hand until a long, jagged blade was pointing directly at them.

"So, where were we?" Antin asked, smiling with a mouthful of sharp teeth. Everything about him was sharp. His eyes, as usual, flicked around, and also as usual, he kept checking back over his shoulder every few seconds. "Let's see, oh yeah, you guys were just about to tell me what Emmet was after when we were so rudely interrupted."

The three boys behind Antin, their confidence now completely restored, stepped forward, kicking away the litter, snickering.

"What's the matter, your tongues disappear?" one of them joked.

"Heel here says you can make yourself disappear," Antin said to Dexter. "Can you do that?"

Dex shook his head.

"No, I didn't think so," Antin laughed. "But I'm gonna show you how if you don't tell me what I want to know."

"Hey, maybe it's got something to do with them books," suggested another boy. He was short and wide, with arms that hung too far down the length of his legs.

Dex realized Daphna was still holding the books. Her knuckles were white around the spine of the Ledger.

Antin moved toward the twins now. He could see they were immobilized with fear, so he didn't even bother brandishing the knife. "What's up with the books?" he asked, but got no response. Standing right between them now, he said, "You guys look tired. I'm gonna count to three, and if I don't get the truth, the whole truth, and nothing but the truth, I'm gonna help you get some serious sleep."

"The mattress!" Dex and Daphna called this out at exactly the same time.

"What mattress?" Antin demanded.

"In our dad's room," Daphna said, her senses returning, at least in part. "That's what Emmet was after. It's full of money."

"Show me."

"Upstairs," said Dex.

"Show me."

Dex swallowed dryly, then led Antin upstairs as the other boys herded Daphna along behind. When the group entered Milton's room, Antin said, "If this ain't for real—Eyeballs, check it out."

Eyeballs, a wiry boy with purple hair and bulging eyes, ripped the sheets and covers off the bed. When he noticed the zipper on the far side, he moved around and squatted to open it.

Then he screamed.

"What?" Antin shouted. "What!" In a sudden, terrifying motion, he whipped the blade to Dex's throat.

"There must be a million bucks in here!" Eyeballs yowled. No one was absolutely sure what he'd said, though, because his head was halfway into the opening. But then a bundle of bills came flying. It landed at Antin's feet.

It was like a piñata had been broken at a toddler's unsupervised birthday party. Antin and his hobbled cronies hurled themselves over the bed. Money went flying.

It took longer than it should have, but eventually Dex and Daphna realized they'd been forgotten. Slowly, they inched out of the room. Without running—neither had the energy anyway—they slipped carefully through the living room and, clasping their books to their chests, stumbled out through the still-open front door and into the evening's dwindling light.

CHAPTER FOURTEEN
Still Not a Bad Man

Though the twins were nearly out on their feet, both saw him the moment they lurched onto their porch. A man in a rumpled black suit, tall and thin, with a day's worth of stubble on his slender face, was standing behind a tree across the street. He swiveled sideways and pressed himself behind the trunk when he realized they were looking his way.

Dex and Daphna exchanged a droopy-eyed glance they both understood to mean, *Now what? We don't care.* Wordlessly, they agreed to pretend they hadn't seen anything and shuffled off.

They couldn't pretend for long. The man, who must have realized he'd been seen, started blatantly following them. He wasn't chasing them, though, which was fortunate since there was no way either of the twins could outrun him. They couldn't outrun their father right now.

The man walked down the road behind them, calmly, like he just happened to be taking a stroll exactly where they were going. Of course, that was impossible for many reasons, not the least of which was neither Dex nor Daphna had the slightest idea where they were headed.

Being followed so openly grew increasingly unnerving. The twins looked back every few seconds, like Antin. Since they lacked the energy to run for it, they began making sudden, random turns around the Village streets and doubling back whenever it seemed least likely.

The man was undeterred. He took each and every turn they did. He cut between houses, crossed yards, and circled garages right behind them, though he continued to make no effort to catch up. The twins' heads bowed lower and lower as they trudged on. Their steps slowed; their knees wobbled; their chests heaved. Still, they didn't stop. They moved by instinct alone.

Instinct, and enough weaving through the neighborhood, eventually brought them in sight of the R & R. Dex and

Daphna, both of whom were considering just turning around and letting the man kill them if that's what he really wanted to do, stumbled toward the entrance. They staggered through the automatic doors and dragged themselves down the hall. Falling all over each other, they pitched themselves into their father's room.

Milton was sleeping. Daphna called her dad's name several times, and she even shuffled herself over to shake him by the shoulder, but he wouldn't wake up. He slept soundly, his face flush with a healthy, ruddy glow.

Dex had immediately dumped himself onto the couch, so Daphna joined him, and the two slumped into each other, breathing heavily and staring indifferently up at the TV, which was showing a muted news talk show. They felt nothing except bone-deep exhaustion. Neither was the slightest bit curious about their stalker, though they both knew he'd be walking in the door at any moment.

Two pairs of speckled green eyes began to close.

Sleep, precious, golden, glorious sleep was finally coming, but sure enough, just before the twins passed out, the door opened and the man walked in.

Dex and Daphna sat up and looked at him with blank, utterly indifferent stares. The man had olive skin and twitchy fingers. He looked at the twins, but quickly turned to their father. "Mr. Milton Wax?" he demanded, but Milton didn't respond. "Mr. Milton Wax!" he repeated, raising his voice. "You will explain at once your involvement with my grandfather, and you will return his papers to me this very instant!"

"He won't wake up," said Daphna. "He's on medication."

"And he's kind of messed up in the head," Dex added, not caring how it sounded.

The man strode to the bedside and shook Milton by the shoulder, just as Daphna had done. As predicted, Milton didn't wake up, though he did shift around and mutter, "Adem Tarik—Adem Tarik—I—I—" His voice was so ragged that it was becoming difficult to make the words out. The man seemed to understand, though. He drew back, looking alarmed. "I am not bad man," Milton croaked, "I—I—am—"

"Who is this 'Adem Tarik'!" the man demanded.

"No idea," Dex lied. "He made it up. He says that name all the time."

"We told you," Daphna repeated, "he's got psychological problems. He's got a—disorder."

The man sighed, mightily. He looked, the twins suddenly noticed, rather exhausted himself. He walked across the room and sat down in what had been Latty's chair and put his head in his hands.

"You're Fikret Cihan," Dex said. "You own the Coffee House."

The man looked up, surprised. "Yes, how do you know this?"

"I was the one who sent that e-mail," Dex explained, "the one that was all jumbled up. It was an accident."

Cihan looked at him, amazed and appalled. "It was nothing?" he said, almost pleading. "Random typing, you say?"

"Adem Tarik—" Milton crackled, "Adem Tarik—I—I—am—"

"I see now," said Cihan, massaging his nose. "It was one lunatic meeting another." He chuckled briefly, sounding slightly mad himself.

"But, why were you following us?" Daphna asked. "Why are you here? You must have been traveling all day and night."

Cihan ran a hand through his short black hair. "My grandfather," he explained, "spent the last sixty years of his life copying a book, a book full of nonsense and rubbish. My God! Is that the book right there?" It was sitting on Milton's food tray, on top of the Ledger.

"Ah," said Dex, "I don't know."

Cihan rose and took the book without asking permission, then flipped through it with a mournful look on his face. Dex couldn't even pretend to have the wherewithal to stop him. "Did your father give this to you?" Cihan's voice took on a threatening edge.

"Ah, yeah," Dex said. "He told me it was worthless. I like old books, so—"

"I—I—Adem—"

Cihan looked at Milton and heaved another defeated sigh. He turned to the twins again but didn't hand the book back. Dex and Daphna looked at each other, nervously.

"Your father came into my Coffee House," he said, "asking about this Adem Tarik, and my grandfather gave him this book. It was like a miracle after all these years! There was never a sign such a thing would ever be. How long had I hoped to spend time with my grandfather! I was overjoyed when your father left, but things did not go the way I'd hoped."

"What do you mean?" asked Daphna.

"He was beside himself when he realized your father had not taken away the copies," Cihan explained. "I was too excited by this miracle to remember them, but your father, he left me his card. My grandfather forced me to mail every page at once, and at great expense.

"Once they were gone, he got weak. I think he only stayed alive to make those copies. He died the morning I received your message, and since it was just like that book and those copies, it made me suspicious. I thought perhaps your father did know my grandfather, and that the message was in code. My family once took quite seriously the idea that the book was in a code of some kind. Many years were wasted in hopes of interpreting it. I flew all the way here to retrieve the book and notebooks and demand your father tell me what he knows. But now I see I have wasted my time."

Dex and Daphna both thought Cihan was about to hand the book back. Dex even put his hand out, but it didn't happen.

"I've got some bad news for you," Daphna said. Cihan looked at her with an expression that seemed to say he expected no other kind. "All the copies," she said, "we sort of burned them."

"We thought they might make Dad crazier," Dex put in.

Cihan's shoulders sank further, and he dropped his head into his hands again. He stayed that way for long time, long enough for Dex and Daphna to silently urge each other to figure out how to get the book back. Before either could think of a way, Cihan got to his feet.

"Fine. Good," he said. When he saw the confused look on the twins' faces, he elaborated. "You've done me a favor," he explained. "Who knows, I may have become obsessed myself. I could never have destroyed those papers myself. Here, please keep this infernal book too," he added, handing the book back to Dexter. "Destroy it if you like. I don't care."

"Ah, thanks." Dex took the book back, gripping it with both hands.

Cihan shook his head again. "Every day, people come to my Coffee House asking for me to help them make sense of their lives," he said. "For generations, my family has survived on such hopes, and I once believed that the riddles of the Universe could be solved. But the truth is that our lives are incomprehensible intersections of unfathomable events and meaningless coincidences. I've been arrogant and foolish to think I could decipher the pattern of even my own insignificant destiny. Let me give you a piece of advice, children," he added. "Thinking is suffering."

"Tarik—Adem—I—I—" Milton droned.

The twins could see this was a deeply troubled person, but they couldn't exactly disagree with his pronouncement.

It took a moment, but a word jumped out at Dex. "You said coincidences," he said. "Do you mean my father coming into your Coffee House and getting that book?"

"Indeed," said Cihan. "But I will not seek to understand why my grandfather chose your father after so many years when so many thousands of people passed through our doors."

"But it must have something to do with Adem Tarik, right?" Dex said. "Hearing my father ask about him must've meant something to him."

"This is impossible."

"Why do you say that?" Daphna asked.

"My grandfather was deaf. He'd been so for many years."

"Oh."

Cihan looked at Daphna, apparently expecting further questions. When none came, he said, "Remember what I told you: Thinking is suffering. I bid you farewell." With head down, Cihan strode from the room. It sounded like he ran into someone in the hall. "Excuse me, Ma'am," was the last thing the twins heard him say. Then he was gone.

"Adem Tarik—I—I—" Milton croaked.

The twins stared at their father. They'd uncovered so many secrets since they'd first sat right where they were now, listening to the same words just after they'd arrived at the R & R. But there were so many more.

"Dex," Daphna said after a few minutes, "I don't get it."

"Me neither," Dex mumbled in reply. "I give up."

But Daphna had the notion something critical had just been revealed. "Dad went into the Coffee House," she said, trying to grasp the sequence of events as she now understood them. "Then he asked that guy about Adem Tarik, right?"

"Right," Dex agreed, though he was hearing Daphna more than listening to her. What he was thinking about was sleep.

"And then his grandfather flips out and forces the book on Dad, right?"

"Right."

Almost on cue, Milton croaked, "Adem Tarik—Adem Tarik—I am—I—"

"But he just said his grandfather was deaf," Daphna pressed. "So he couldn't've heard Dad ask about anything. That's what we assumed happened, I guess. I mean, why wouldn't we?"

"And?" Now Dexter was getting plain annoyed. Why wasn't Daphna letting him pass out?

"Dexter," Daphna insisted. "The old guy saw Dad, then he gave him the book. He saw Dad, then he gave him Adem Tarik's book. And Dad was actually there to get it, whether he knew it or not."

"It makes no sense," Dexter protested, "not unless he thought Dad actually was—"

Suddenly, Milton sat bolt upright in his bed, his eyes shocked wide. "I AM—" he roared in a booming, crystal clear voice, "I AM ADEM TARIK!"

The twins' blood froze.

"*I am Adem Tarik!*" their father proclaimed again, sounding amazed and relieved. Then he hopped out of the bed with no sign of pain whatsoever.

Horror-struck, the twins watched as he stretched his back and flexed his arms and legs. His posture was perfect. He looked as agile as a man of twenty.

"I AM ADEM TARIK!" he declared to the mirror on a dresser. "My, oh my, oh my, oh my! All these years, trying to remember! My, oh my, oh my!" He bent over to touch his toes and noticed the twins on the couch, staring at him like imbeciles. "Ah!" he said. "I'm not alone."

"All—all this time," Daphna stuttered, "you—you were looking for—yourself."

"You found the book sixty years ago and made Fikret Cihan's grandfather copy it for you," Dex said. "You kept going back to Turkey, because some part of you knew it was there."

"Very impressive," said Adem Tarik. "And who might you two be?"

"I—I'm—Dexter," Dex croaked, cut to the quick.

"And you, young lady?"

"Daphna. You're our father."

"I HAVE CHILDREN? *Living* children?"

"Yes," Dexter snarled. "We didn't die like the ones you had with Mrs. Tapi and Mrs. Kunyan and Mrs. Deucalion. You married them all, but you ditched them when their babies died."

"My goodness," Tarik said, grinning in an awful way his kids had never seen before. His face had lost its wrinkles, and his speckled brown eyes seemed filled with sparks. He looked like he was getting younger and healthier right in front of them. "You two know quite a lot about me," he added. "I must say it's quite flattering. Please, tell me more."

"You'd been planning all along to get the book back when you had kids who turned thirteen!" Daphna shouted, her rage returning despite her near-total exhaustion. She wasn't really addressing her father. She just wanted these secrets revealed once and for all, even if only for hers and Dexter's ears. "That's why you always talked about our thirteenth birthday being such a big deal!"

"When it got close," Dex realized, "you remembered just enough to find that coffee shop. The old man recognized you and gave it—"

"Wait a moment," Tarik interrupted. "Are you two *thirteen?*"

"That's why you brought the book home just when Rash and everyone else came for us!" Dex cried. "It's *all* been about our thirteenth birthday. There've been no coincidences in anything that's happened!"

"And I see you've got my book!" Tarik replied, delighted. "Probably still useless, though, no? What am I doing here?"

"You killed our mother," Dexter growled.

"Oh, thank goodness! The last thing I remember was trying to shove her and that annoying assistant of hers over a ledge in my caves. The caves! I got hit in the head, didn't I? Oh, how absurd! No matter! I killed them both."

"You didn't kill—" Daphna started to say, but Dex shot her a dire look. Why should they tell him he didn't kill Latty? Why should they tell him anything? And Latty! *What about Latty?*

"I'm afraid I did," Milton said, "and I'm sure I seem like some kind of monster to you. I shouldn't act so callous. She was your mother, after all. I'm sorry for your loss. But you must understand, children. I am not a bad man. I have a plan, and if you'll allow me, I'd like to explain why what I did had to be done. I want to share my plan with you—the most ambitious plan ever conceived! When you understand, you'll want to help me, and it seems you are ready to do so. I promise you: We are going to do great and glorious things together!"

Daphna spat on the floor at her father's feet. "That's what we think of your plan!" she snapped. "We know what those poor kids were told—kids who trusted you—that they'd be making Heaven on Earth! Well, if your kind of Heaven includes murdering people, you can go to Hell!"

"I see," said Adem Tarik, apparently unperturbed by this venomous outburst. "You did not express my aspirations quite correctly. Bear in mind, children, that words matter, even the smallest among them. If you'll allow me, I'd like to fetch some other materials which will convince you that—"

"Too late," Dex said, his growl turning triumphant. "We got the copies. And we burned every last one of them."

Adem Tarik's face went dark and his smile dropped away. "How very unfortunate," he said, turning his attention to the book still in Dexter's hand.

Dexter clutched it to his chest and took a step backward.

The twins were far beyond too tired to think what they should do, but before they were forced to decide one way or another, the door flew open, banging the wall behind it.

Startled, everyone turned.

Fikret Cihan strode back into the room and directly up to Dexter, his face flushed and perspiring. "No!" he told Dex, as if they were in the middle of an argument. "I will not let my grandfather's life mean nothing! I will find the truth in this book of secrets!"

Dex was not equipped to handle any new surprises, so when Fikret Cihan reached for the Book of Nonsense, he did not resist. Fikret simply took it out of his hand. Then, without another word, he turned back to the door.

Which is when Adem Tarik grabbed him by the throat and lifted him, with one hand, straight into the air.

"Nooo!" Daphna screamed. "Stop!"

Fikret made sickening gurgling noises while his legs kicked wildly, but uselessly, at Tarik's shins.

But he didn't relinquish the book.

Your Word, Dex! Use your Word! Make him stop!

It took a moment for Dex to summon it, but once he dredged it from the fog in his brain, he shouted the Word as loudly as he could.

For a moment, the twins thought it worked. Adem Tarik turned and looked directly at Dexter with wide eyes—and he seemed to freeze that way—staring at him. Fikret stopped struggling and gasped for air.

But the moment did not last.

Tarik turned his attention back to Fikret, who flailed and gurgled again. Dex shouted his Word another time. Then he shouted it again. And then again. "It's not work—!" he cried, but he was cut off by Daphna, who was now screaming her Word.

If he was going to choke someone, she thought, *he could choke too.*

Again, Tarik turned, this time to look at Daphna, but only for an instant.

It wasn't working, so Daphna opened her mouth to shriek her Word loud enough to burst her father's eardrums, but the most horrifying sound she ever heard closed it.

Fikret Cihan's neck snapping.

Adem Tarik dropped him to the floor like a side of beef.

Dexter and Daphna stood where they were, beyond their capacity to accept what they'd just seen.

Tarik leaned over and plucked The Book of Nonsense from Fikret Cihan's dead hands and gave it back to Dexter, who took it dumbly. Then he walked to the window next to the bed and slid it open.

Then he came back and lifted Fikret's body off the floor like it was a ragdoll. He carried it to the window, and after a quick look through, shoved the dead man outside.

Tarik put a leg through, but paused to look at his stupefied children. "I remember you now," he told them. "Dexter, given your academic record, your lackluster delivery of that Word is hardly surprising. But Daphna, *really.* I'm very disappointed." The he added, "Children, I'll be in touch."

And with that, he climbed through the window and was gone.

CHAPTER FIFTEEN
Latty

The twins looked at each other through barely open eyes. Neither spoke. Neither had anything to say.

Finally, Daphna turned away. She grabbed her bag and shuffled off into the bathroom. Dex closed the window and changed into his pajamas while she was in there, then climbed into his cot. When Daphna came out, she turned the light off and climbed into hers.

Brother and sister lay in the dark without talking for several minutes.

They did not fall asleep.

"*Latty,*" Daphna whispered some indeterminate amount of time later. "*She knew the truth all along. She told us she saw him trying to save her, but the truth is she saw him pushing her. She—She—*"

"She took advantage of him forgetting who he was so she could stay with us as his assistant," Dex said. His eyes were open, staring into shadows. "She was protecting us. It's just like Ruby said, remember? Keep your friends close, but your enemies closer."

"But not too close. That's why she encouraged him to be a scout, to travel around and stay away from us until she learned his stupid plan. And that's why she doesn't like Evelyn, because if Dad married her, she wouldn't be able to look after us."

"That's why she got so scared he'd remember. That's why she cleared out all the pictures of her and took off. If he finds out she didn't fall, and that she knows the truth, he'll kill her for sure. She—she—"

"Loves us."

"Everything makes sense now, Daphna. He was in great shape before the accident, until he forgot who he was. Now he remembers, and it's coming back. Who knows how old he really is."

"You were right all along. Dad never cared about us at

all."

"If I was right," Dex admitted, "it was for the wrong reasons. Have two stupider people ever walked the face of the Earth? He's been telling us he was Adem Tarik over and over for *days*. All that stuff he was saying in his sleep, that he was failing, that he'd done something wrong. He was failing to carry out his great and glorious plan."

"Latty!" the twins wailed in the dark. *"What have we done?"*

About the Author

David Michael Slater is an acclaimed author of books for children, teens, and adults. He teaches English to seventh and eighth graders, but you will not be required to take a test after reading this book. David lives in Reno, Nevada with his wife and son. You can learn more about David and his work at www.davidmichaelslater.com.